AGE

BOOKS BY HORTENSE CALISHER

NOVELS

False Entry
Textures of Life
Journal from Ellipsia
The New Yorkers
Queenie
Standard Dreaming
Eagle Eye
On Keeping Women
Mysteries of Motion
The Bobby-Soxer

NOVELLAS AND SHORT STORIES

In the Absence of Angels
Tale for the Mirror
Extreme Magic
The Railway Police and the Last Trolley Ride
The Collected Stories of Hortense Calisher
Saratoga, Hot

AUTOBIOGRAPHY

Herself

AGE

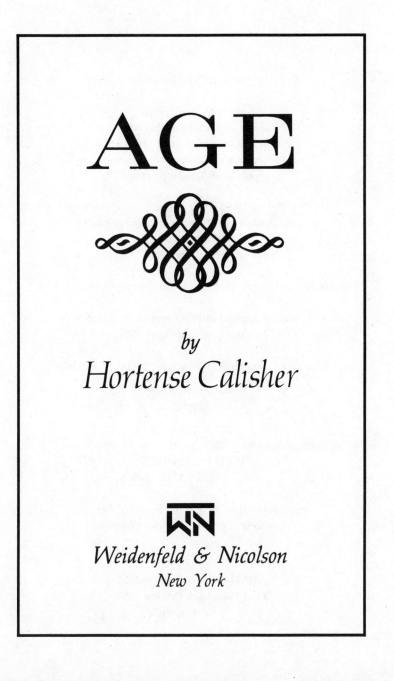

by
Hortense Calisher

Weidenfeld & Nicolson
New York

Published by Weidenfeld & Nicolson, New York
A Division of Wheatland Corporation
841 Broadway
New York, New York 10003-4793

Published in Canada by General Publishing Company, Ltd.

Originally published in hardcover by Weidenfeld &
Nicolson, New York, in 1987.

Library of Congress Cataloging-in-Publication Data

Calisher, Hortense.
Age.

I. Title.
PS3553.A4A7   1987   813′.54   86-34005
ISBN 1-55584-132-5
ISBN 1-55584-371-9 (pbk.)

Manufactured in the United States of America
This book is printed on acid-free paper

Designed by Helen Barrow
First Hardcover Edition 1987
First Paperback Edition 1989
1   3   5   7   9   10   8   6   4   2

I SUPPOSE most couples the age of Rupert and me are not expected to be still compelled by sex. He and I still go on, side by side in our delicately fading pleasure-harness. Our performance is like memory, sometimes faint, sometimes strong. Often dampened by the daily rhythms, or refreshed by the slightest novelty. As a couple in our seventies, with me four years ahead of him, we are said not to be too bad a business to the eyes of those in the rear.

We ourselves see every change, as in autumn one does. He tells me that my head, hawked by so much architectural seeing, and set on shoulders stiffened into the drawing-board curve, is now like those marble busts with flows of serpentine hair that one meets in the corridors of palaces newly opened to the public. To me his tallness is still romantically stooped, and under his pebble-colored thatch the fine features, small for a man of his height, can still pinken like a boy's. Our naked bodies are more of a match now, brought to resemblance by the Palladian lines of aging. Yet to me the aquiline of his nose is still a kind of physical poetry. While he says that the slack underside of my upper arm and forearm, when pulled, is like a Greek wave etched by an artist adept at those border patterns.

"Little iambs of skin—" he says, as his finger slides. But then, we are both helped by our professions. He is the poet—who no longer writes much. I am the architect—who no longer builds.

So we reminisce with our flesh—and stretch our limbs toward the present. Nor do we lie to ourselves. We are also making gestures against death—only from a vantage nearer than for most. What bothers us deepest is that one of us will inevitably be left behind.

But although we once met the writer Arthur Koestler and his wife in London—he originally a friend of Rupert's former wife, Gertrude, who still lives there—the double suicide of the Koestlers, reasonable as it may have been to them, still seems to us dreadful. "She so much the younger—" Rupert said at the time. "And still in health." In our case, so are we both, and in genes about equivalent—the nineties even possible, we dare to think—if modern stress permits.

Yet, like any duo, we cannot hope to die in absolute yoke, dropping together in the brown furrow some hardy October. And as dying goes we are each in our own way opposed to it. Take us singly, and we are rebels on more than one score. Only together do we grow meek.

So—we have decided. From now on we will each keep an almanac. For company—to the one of us who survives. To be read by him or me—only afterward.

"You start—" Rupert said. "Pen-and-ink comes easier to you."

We smile—at the old joke. Pen-and-ink is literally his medium. Older though I am, I have rarely touched either, having gone straight from kindergarten crayon to a child's typewriter, not at all a toy and with a circular central dial even analogous to today's electronic "daisy," made for me by an architect uncle, when I was five. What Rupert means is that the words come easier to me because that is not my profession, and because I use a word processor. "And that will encourage *me*—" he adds. Back to poems as well? He doesn't mind my knowing of his dearth, rather expecting me to.

So of course, I begin at once. Throughout our thirty-five years together he has been the encourager. I don't tell him that even in front of this easy-working screen the shoulders he admires for their marble grow more so each day.

He knows. Dear Rupert, I write as we agreed. I begin. But I refuse to think of you as possibly to die—or dead.

SO—SHE THINKS it begins? But in the white and red scrawls of our brains hasn't a diamond-point stylus begun swinging from each to each the first day? And so blending that except for pronouns and other minutiae, an outsider would not otherwise distinguish what I write from what she will; the confessions will be so much the same? By now there is also that fine aping which spins its thread between those who share time, sperm, and interest. Open our skulls and you might find blood-thickets identical—only mine now all blueprints, and in hers a poem.

Otherwise we don't look enough alike to bore people, as so many of the long-married do.

"Saved from that—" Gemma laughs, "by two rickety Mexican divorces."

In which to this day none of the four parties involved quite believes. Because of that, under legal suggestion, each of us signed away any claim to the putative estate of the former spouse. Then, as we thought at the time, those two would drop away and out of our lives except for the stray bulletin—as we would from theirs. Gertrude—perhaps still working for one or the other London publisher, meanwhile pursuing, one after the other, her bitter, darkly Freudian love-bouts. Arturo, from his picture a man with the sweet round face often found on the easy hedonist—in his case a father who gave up all rights to and support for his and Gemma's two young daughters with an airy promise to "send for them now and then"—did go back to Siena to be "the young Count" again to his family's servant-girls, although he was already in his fifties, and worked in a bank.

In our own modest joint estate, Gemma's and mine, what is it that one can neither sign away nor leave behind? Circumstance.

I was a Long Island brewer's son, who, after a second-rate but not sinister prep school, refused college and went to Wyoming instead to work as a cowpuncher. In the areas of horses, girls, and campfire kinship I served happily, after eight years returning to the East minus two front teeth, plus some mended bones, and with a head still intent on certain nightingales I hadn't found out West. In hopes of song outside myself, I married a raven-haired staff member of a literary review, a woman whom I saw as a slim reed swayed by the winds of literature, not, as was the case, merely quivering from the latest critic's bed.

Gertrude was one of those for whom sex appeared to be the path both to spiritual discovery and to a livelihood, the priority of either being arguable. Her very history compelled toward her lovers like me, and had a magical interest for outsiders as well. There the verdict was that she was not a femme fatale, since all her men eventually got away.

I was the primitive talent she found before others did. Beware of those like me; we often turn out not to be primitive enough, even to ourselves. By day I worked in the circus or kennel end of the theater, as anything from stuntman to animal expert on such necessaries as dogs in plays and elephants in opera. So I was still toutable as nature's man. By night I did walk-ons as a beginning poet on the party-stages of those marathon talkers who kept the bivouacs going for the wars of art.

Seven years of that—and enjoyable.

"You take what comes, Rupert," Gemma says, "and squeeze the good from it."

But Rupert is aware that any healthy man, also reason-ably in pocket, who doesn't enjoy his thirties, is a dolt. And perhaps any woman. Though a man cannot truly know how women view the curves of circumstance, I do know that it is in that view, more than in any curve of hip or of inner egg, that they least resemble us.

Still, Gemma had forty years of herself to herself—or not to herself, as she may see it—the last twenty-two as Arturo's wife and her girls' mother, in the synecdoch-ically plump county of Westchester, New York.

Gemma, when you read this you will have to look that up. I plan for you to—and in this same instant, relent. *Synecdoche* means taking the part or parts for the whole—and that is certainly what the suburbs do. So let us share, postmortem, a joke we would have enjoyed in a joint life. For I write this as from the dead, sure that you will survive us, our duality, better than me. Meanwhile, let me talk you gently toward me, through whatever time you have left.

Did I know at once, when Gemma and I met, that she was to be my survivor on an island formed by all the years to come? Back when Arturo, a teacher of art at the "American" college courses in Perugia, began to court his blue-eyed, blonde Italo-American student, his Tus-can family had thought her North Italian in ancestry. When this only child of a Bridgeport, Connecticut, con-tractor was discovered to be of Sicilian stock, there was at first the devil to pay—all rosied over when Arturo disclosed that she was also Jewish—like them. An only child—Gemma had said to them winsomely—how could I be Catholic? And the Count, Arturo's father, had turned out to be only a *commendatore* really, a military title derived from his military service with Mussolini in North Africa—and for a Jew doubly devious. But so were some of the dollars made by contractors.

"Brewer's stock is more honest," she sometimes says when we differ about money.

No—only more tediously literal. Though I don't grudge her any fluff or sortie, I swore always to have enough to leave her comfortably provided for.

"What comfort will that be?" she flares. "And I'm older. Give it to me now."

I take her literally. From under the covers I say afterward, "And I'm younger. A gigolo must self-provide."

What she calls my charm is merely the bland, beer garden temperament my family deeded me, along with a one-eighth interest in an oversized house in Garden City, on only one acre of sward. Plus some Teuton jokes which now and then surface in light verse. Little curlicues left over from Shrove Tuesday family revels in the neatly whitewashed basement, where we munched *Fastnacht* crullers and bobbed for apple-luck. No taste for bloodshed except in the *Dämmerung* of Wagner, and easily absorbed by the safe red velvet box-seat of a season ticket. No taste for war, except as goose-stepped to an oompah band that in the spring twiddled on our street. Such an upbringing can be rationalized away. But the optimism is ineradicable.

How I go on. But there's all the time in the world now, my dear, isn't there. I have no logical problem about thinking of you as pre-deceasing me, Gemma. But traumatically I would not have tolerated it. Remember how, when you wanted to let your hair go white, I insisted you keep it the soft brown it had darkened to before graying—and that's my honesty.

What I saw over a quarter of a century ago was the gracile blonde mother of two and supporter of three— for Arturo, ensconced at home in a country where even a bravura painter is excused from working during siestas adhered to as rigorously as when he had briefly been employed at the bank, now found he loved his girls too much to let them skimp along on American culture. Commandeering their presence in the name of Italy and an ancient house where they could have a father for free—both arguments that softened Gemma—he wooed them for longer and longer visits, from which only substantial ransom rescued them back to her.

I saw a woman who seemed to me all heart-shaped— face, breasts, and hips—above those long Aryan legs that sometimes do disconcertingly grow right out of the Old Testament.

"I'm a builder," you said. "I never graduated as an architect."

Later I would make you go back and get your degree.

"I'm a pretty good poet," I said. Indeed they sometimes let me teach it—at the convent school near the animal-boarding farm I now owned and, according to some, had made almost beautiful enough for people to live on.

Circumstance—yes, men speak differently of it.

"I'd give a lot to work as a landscape gardener," you said. "But that takes acreage. I and the people I know out here—we haven't it."

"I always wanted to rewrite Virgil's _Georgics,_" I said.
"But that takes acreage too."

We stared at one another. We were in the house of a
famous conductor and his wife who had opened their
door to the kind of benefit rally for a radical cause at
which only the well-heeled can safely appear.

"Everything here is down in black and white," I said.
"The people. The money. And the opinions."

The people here, Gemma said, looked to her like loz-
enges. As I was to discover, she always saw people in
shapes. Those here, she said, were oblongs all of the
same size, with very sharp corners.

"Maybe it's their opinions sticking out," I said. "Like
Kleenex, from the pockets of well-tended children."

"But someone else blows their noses for them," she
said.

We stared again—remember?

"We're only on the local guest-list of sympathizers,
you and I," I said then. "Or else we have a lover here.
Have you?"

"I did," she said, looking across the room. "Have
you?"

"As a matter of fact—" I said, "—not yet."

So should we leave—I said—before the speeches?
"We're not that talented."

"They'll have caviar afterward," you said. "They always do." But you were smiling, and the smile was heart-
shaped too.

"So shall we," I said. We were always both of us so
good at repartee.

So we joined hands, and left the neosophisticate life.
I sold the farm, for a flat in the city. You sold your half

of the firm in White Plains for a drawing board. Plus the opportunity to landscape a forty-foot city garden, southern exposed. And so we entered that bourgeoisie to which every loving couple of long duration willy-nilly belongs.

Repartee is still the spice of it, and the daily jaunt. But at the farther end is this record. Where nobody will answer.

We've not done badly, Gemma and I. Even under the aspect of the stars a decent poet and architect must be of some worth to the millenniums. Or of no worth at all, except as the ash a universe must have.

Still—the cosmos must cede us our dying. At a stroke, or inch by inch. And the extra inch Gemma and I ask to add—inch of grace, if not of credit, minute stretch of will, if not of joy—is this record.

I think to myself—is this the acreage? The space we wanted—and now earn?

I SAID to Rupert: "What shall we be calling it, this account? Oh—just between ourselves?"

"Let's not name it," he said, and we both fell silent, remembering how in the first pride of accession he tried to name his farm, as people do—to wear as a signet on notepaper and cherish in speech. And how he could never find the one name to satisfy all the needs, and so ended by calling it "the house."

"Just between ourselves?" he said. "For whom else is it?"

To refer to, I meant—as we go along with it. I'll need that. I'm not like he is, always scratching on alone.

He senses that. "We can have different names," he said, like to a child. "From time to time." And I think how brave of him, and how foolish, to refer to time—ours—as of indefinite length.

"When did you first begin to think of your lifetime as limited?" I said. "Oh—not the cliché way—but in the real grain."

"When did I know I was mortal for sure?"

When he's cornered he searches his pockets. The children used to watch him put out penny after penny after penny, in a straight line. "Not sure I ever have. What I retain is how it feels—every young day—that one is destined to live forever. Like those dreams that are all one intense blue."

He grins then—what I call his triolet grin—the smirk he wears coming out of his studio, after he has written one of those. In a triolet the first line has to rhyme with the fourth and seventh. There are only eight. And that last line—which has to rhyme with the second—has to come true, and yet casual. "Like the only bong possible." Or sometimes he does those acrostic poems in which the first letters of each line, when read vertically, spell a sentiment.

At times I hate his wordplay. It doesn't help that so does he. They're poems for xylophones, he says, not for violins. And they sap the real stuff. I can always tell from his conversation—with others or with me—when he's been doing them.

"Oh you know me"—he says now—"I can never remember what I forget."

There isn't a couple alive that doesn't develop some kind of verbal venom—his phrase, of course. It comes of the interlocking—even when one wants never to be sundered—of small habits that should be learned and accepted—the other person's—but never fully are. He's kinder about this than me. Or less callous. When I want my blueprints spread on the dining table, I *want*—to accompanying shrieks if he clears for lunch. But when he doesn't empty his all-day tea leaves—I sulk. Housewives develop certain venoms of gesture, I tell him. "But it's no help—that we are ashamed of them."

He answers that he and I must write down the daily impatiences too: These are part of what we are. The one who reads would know otherwise that the picture is false.

"What difference will that make?" I say. "It won't be my picture you lack."

He grips my wrists as roughly as he once used to. I feel their gauntness all the more because of his knotted hands, each of whose bumps and blotches I plot like a changing landscape.

"You must not believe only in *your* death," he says. "You must learn to believe in *mine.*"

And so we face each other, openmouthed. For each of us the dilemma is the same.

WHAT IS DEATH to her and me now—an aphrodisiac?

That, now that I had said it out plain, the two of us, a woman approaching seventy-seven and a man seventy-three, should close jaws, eyes, bend our knees, back ourselves against a wall, and make love standing up?

We did that a lot when we first met. We hadn't done so in years. Often in bed we make love without climax now, or barely, and do not ask "Did you?" afterward.

This time, as I feel the rise and certainty in both of us, I see, past her shoulder, the small carpet-covered set of three steps we use as a kitchen ladder to the storage closets above. Then we shuddered toward the great cry.

We should be stood up in St. Pat's as a miracle—neither of us said. The flesh dripped, and I marveled. She put her wet cheek in my neck—and I nodded.

Afterward I said: "What are they, really. That set of steps?" She brings things home. They melt into usage. "Is it a prayer stool?"

"Could be. Or else steps to get into one of those high tester-beds."

Then we laugh, and have ourselves coffee black as the midwinter ice on a lake on an animal farm used to be, and cheese smacking of the best cholesterol, and grapes.

"You look so pretty," I say, mouth full. "Maybe I'll let you leave your hair white."

She kisses the backs of my hands. She's always looking at them. She waves at the little ladder. "Next time, we'll kneel."

HE SAYS I keep him from seeing himself, and us, as too heroic. "I always did think the old were the real heroes," he says.

And now—they're us. I think that for both of us.

"To be under imminent sentence," he says. "And threading a needle."

Sewing the button, I smirk. My eyes are good. None of our family has ever had cataracts. "That's our function. Women."

"To thread? Or to be antiheroic?"

"To be antiheroic—heroines."

Repartee!

But now and then we sly out each other's hurts—at least the old chronic ones. I am a great complainer on the subject of the neck. He knows each of my muscle crackings and is a connoisseur of the heat lamp and the traction apparatus, as well as an amateur masseur. But that other inner Babel of body sounds and heart tricks—all new arrivals crashing the tap-dance rehearsal without their union cards—these I keep to myself. And so, I suppose, does he. Or I assume he has five years less of them.

Until one day, when we are standing between two reflecting mirror-walls in a gallery show of environmental art—dribbled earth, bow-tied walls, and quicksand views of us spectators—I find out that he too has a neck.

He has stopped dead in his tracks, though we are supposed to tread across that earth—and spoil our shoes in it if we are wearing uptown suede. We aren't. In the silly-mirror I see him touch his forehead. His head is alop.

"Rupert! What?"

That's all we appear to have to say these days: What?

He only told me because he was caught off his guard—by the environment. "Like a black-and-white parasol. Opened right between my eyes. And shook out its frills like Op-art. Moving in ripples."

"Oh—that—" I manage to say. "Dead between the

eyes? Like a paramecium in drag? I've had it. Stand still. It'll go."

The line of people behind us moved on without us, not sparing us some dirty looks. We are from another constituency of the environment—I thought of telling them. One foot out, one foot in.

"It's gone," he said. "I've had it before."

"Why didn't you tell me?"

He knew I knew why, so didn't answer.

But now *I* am the amateur.

I took us home in a cab—ten blocks. Those minor habit changes—sudden cabs, untoward purse-fumblings, a sense that one has talked too much, or else been silent without knowing it—these are the scariest.

Nothing—Rupert's CAT scan said, and the doctor also. What they call an "incident." Not the same, I gather, as—an event.

Rupert does not remember any of it.

I have always been greedy for events. Recently, it has seemed to me, and even to Rupert who has always been less dependent on them, that what with our one remaining daughter so far off and friends going for good—we haven't had enough of them.

Now—I don't know.

FOOD HAS ALWAYS been our joint responsibility. She has taught me to cook a little at her side, and now that she can't carry I often shop alone, though on occasion she likes to come along to help select.

"You two are the most *selecting* parents I know," Christina said, walking through our odd series of rooms again after so long, the year she came back from Italy to live with us and attend the Lincoln School a last year before college—for neither of which her father would pay. The elder child is not always the brightest, but she is—although to her father the infant son he and Gemma lost prematurely will always be in question.

"Oh yes," I said, "we are very select." Naturally she didn't get the pun, being so rusty in English, but it wouldn't take that girl long. I could see how our bare floors, small rugs, some of them only rag, and windows full of sky at the top half and showing the genre scenes of our side street at the bottom, must seem to her, after her father's place, or rather her grandparents', which I imagine as all leftover gilt, mock-antique damask, and the rippled "waterfall"-effect furniture of the 1940s Italian middle class. Although that was Rome as I knew it, not Tuscany. Our paintings are good, two or three thin-framed oils or watercolors to a room, each bought on installment until it was ours to hang. And often the work of a friend. Funny—how of all our group it was invariably the painters who became most famous, though of course not beyond their just deserts. Even at fifteen, Christina approved of their works in an awed way that made me suspect she already knew how much too good for us—for our means, that is—our little collection now was.

Of course she might already have known the names of some. Her father had an American crony over there who supplied all the art historians with slides of U.S. art, and living here and the Lincoln School would do the rest. We allowed her to choose a picture for her own room, and she chose the Reginald Marsh—one of his lovely tarts striding the avenue, full of loose joy. Quiet girl, Christina; I doubt that she would have told her father about it. But the younger girl, Francesca, after her brief Christmas here, must have done so, and he promptly increased the amount of that ransom which has continued almost until this day. Even so, Gemma had always let him hang on to them for longer than he strictly should. "I will not have them bothered!" And he gave them much, she said—a second language and sky, good butter and fruit as well as good manners, schools virtually without drug or sex problems, if otherwise too stringent, and the open heart of Italy itself.

"And the tight purse?"

I only said it that one time; I do not grudge him anything except his fatherhood. The children were a great gift to me, who had none. And the rare fight Gemma and I had at that point did clear the air. Arturo himself, then on the edge of coming here to stay for God knows how long in one of our small spare rooms—for he is shameless—has never since dared. Christina, who heard all, must have shamed *him,* or even refused to let him use her and her sister as leverage—for after that Francesca too more or less came back to us.

They did have lovely manners. I think of Christina out there now in Saudi Arabia, almost in purdah with the other wives of the oil company's executives, and how those manners must stand her in good stead, not only with them and such Saudi people as she might meet, but with herself. Having the baby will help. But is that—and charm—enough for a smart woman? Perhaps—when just remarried at almost forty. Though I have noticed that women museum curators tend to stay younger than their age. Lovely reticent girls like her to begin with, they stay enshrined in those cool halls, maybe tended by the very artifacts under their care, in some sympathy that streams from the long quiet of art.

As for our collection, much of it later went to pay the girls' school fees, when my teaching and Gemma's commissions lessened, and Francesca, as expensively vain as her father, became a problem we paid to stay away. What few artworks I have saved are for Gemma if I die. When I die. But the Marsh is in my will for Christina. Perhaps I should write and say it is hers, when the baby comes. I would have done so long since. But Gemma was so easily wheedled by Francesca. And the good child never asked.

The bad one, all sugar on top, often excused her demands by saying that one may ask anything of those who are lucky in love. I suppose many think that this is really all there is to Gemma and me. No doubt Arturo had so taught the girls—or had tried. Though when Christina did remarry she asked me to give her away—the only reason she was married in church, she said, adding to me in the vestry beforehand, and to Ethan at her side: "He raised me."

Francesca wasn't pressed to come for that second wedding. Her jobs were always shaky at best, even for Rome—if they existed at all, which her mother believed in more than I. But of course she phoned: "Doesn't my sister want a bridesmaid? And I'm dying to meet Ethan."

Recalling Christina's first wedding at home here, and Francesca's sexy monkey-face—and body—tipped outrageously toward all the young men, including the groom, with whom she may have been at a later date successful, I hoped against hope that Gemma would not accede. But of course she did, saying with the deprecation that always hid her joy, "She'll probably arrive without a stitch to her name." Whereupon they would shop for her—Gemma all aglow with that intense mother-daughter intimacy for two days awarded her—as if Francesca was to be the bride.

This was how the girl would set her mother up for the next six months of ruinous conduct, from abortion money for what could only be obtained in—was it France?—"You know Italy, Mother," to a disappearance in Ceylon—or was it Nepal?—in liaison with a supposed member of its royal house. Which did not save her from being ejected from that country for unseemly conduct in one of its temples. Finally came the imprisonment—was it originally in West Germany or East?—for what Gemma still believes was a political action, but I do not. She had to believe in Francesca all the way; I understand that. Or else cut her off—which for Gemma is impossible. Even now.

And I approved. In spite of outbursts of temper, my dear one, I knew I had to. Logic could not be urged. But more than that, you wouldn't have been what you were to me if you had been able to cut people off. The girl herself—lingering on with us for weeks after that first wedding on the excuse that it had snatched her sister from us—I could scarcely address politely. It was her mischief and then her scheme, to make advances to me, in corridors, on picnics, and finally by sneaking into my study nude. I scared her, before I threw her out. "You will pretend to like me—just enough," I said. "From now on. No mischief. No stepfather enmity even, you poor slut. Your mother has had enough to bear."

But a good kind friend we don't see anymore had already come to Gemma to report. "That girl is driving Rupert crazy; he can't get away from her. In your small house." The friend, who is rich, is said still to hear from Arturo, who at the time was her informant, writing her that Francesca had taunted him that she would get to me. *"Nonno"*—she called her father Grandfather because of his years—"want to bet?" She was his favorite. She tortured him too.

So you, Gemma, came to me, to let me hold you, not to reassure you—our faith in each other has been blind, some would say, if well warranted—but to reassure me. "You needn't pretend about her anymore. To like her. Or to conceal from me what she is. I've told her. Be decent when you're here. Or I will cut you off. And I will." And maybe it would have come to that by now if not because of me—if that stony-faced lifer now in Lübeck prison for her murder hadn't done it for you, never revealing why. Her countries confused us until the end.

But that day I said: "You needn't. I've scared her off."

"How? Tell me." You smiled your saddest maternal smile, unaware you wore it. "It might help me."

It wouldn't have. You were never in the army—where killing becomes possible to people like us. Perhaps you knew that. You didn't press. And knew I spoke the truth, and never asked her.

"Hate her for me," was all you said, shivering into me. "I can't."

So, for that second wedding of her sister's, Francesca brought her own equipment—a short white dress you were awed to find was from Fortuny—in whose spiral she moved like its black-eyed core, and the slippery young Roman, with a fat Hapsburg lip and a patrimony to match, who had bought it for her.

"She wants to outshine the bride," I said to you. "She never will." She never could, though Christina was not to blame.

We watched the two of them, each with her chosen man, each of those as different as the two daughters. I saw that you were praying, your eyes blemished with hope. For Francesca was trying to make her friend see the analogy. Of weddings.

But he was watching Christina, straightforward in her gray second wedding-dress, accepting her ring with an upward look that was adornment enough, and I fear he did see what weddings were, his eyes on Christina, his fat lip wet with delight.

"Today—I don't hate," I said.

By then I was older. Who says the middle-aged don't grow? Only the middle-aged themselves, who see that period of their lives as stuck in a swathe of life whose broad ribbon will merely advance, bearing them on. Age knows better. But who will speak for age? Do we only regress? Or do we grow too?

I began this entry intending to talk about the two of us as we are. Instead, all this wandering in the past, telling you what you already know. And telling myself. Do I hope that the story will change, mutate, in the telling? Or do I fear that the aged no longer have events—worth the telling?

You and I inhabit a present in which fewer and fewer
are intimate enough with us to write or phone. Or if so,
not forgetful of it. How does one chronicle that? The
phone is so glumly mum now, and we have two. When
it rings, we vie for it. How to write this side-by-side
libretto, all of whose roles only one of us sings?

Approach it as a poem must be. It was never written
before. My old age has no antecedent. No one's has. Just
as each one's childhood is brewed fresh for the small,
breathless sipper, and to any youth on his first river-
haunted night, youth was never down by the river with
a lover before, so age must sing its own voluntary, in a
chorus of one.

Who speaks for me, sings for me, except this almanac—to an audience of one?

OLD PEOPLE like us are the gardeners of the streets.
Old male shoppers like Rupert especially, carrying home
eggs as if they are also walking on them, their shoulder
bags tremoring. Under the jaunty cap the face is its own
beacon. Or sometimes there is an assistant presence, like
me. These days I watch Rupert as if he is already alone.
In a kind of gymnastic he is not aware of I practice being
his companion ghost. Although I don't believe in
ghosts—or perhaps because of that—I feel reduced in
size, almost Rupert's child. Or perhaps because I cannot
carry.

I note that the greengrocer is still kind, allowing Rupert to hover over the apples to pick out an especially

cheeky flame, the mound of McIntoshes crumbling as he does so. Or to forefinger a scallion bulb with a secret rub, like a lover feeling a vulva. At that I giggle—I'm still alive. Mr. Raso, the vegetable man, doesn't watch us for stealing, as he tells us he has to do now with some senior pensioners. We are long-term customers who he knows shop at the supermarket only for soap powder and other neutrally packaged goods. And he knows I'm Italian, though he doesn't see me at his church. But one day, when I pass there alone, I may hint to him, as I buy a lemon or so, that Rupert suffers from a slight nervous affliction of the hands. Which is true enough—ever since that day in the gallery.

"Poor Raso," my husband says as we leave. "We're his status now."

"Whatever do you mean?"

"Once he was vegetable king of the neighborhood, don't you remember? To have him pick a honeydew for you was like an award. And now he's only the last non-Oriental vegetable stand on the block. And the young don't go to him."

We pass one of those Korean stalls with a salad-bar electric down its center. Neon pimientos, lime and orange melon balls arranged like savory junk, the green fuzz of chicory at the ready, sliced mushrooms jigsawed on pillows of bean curd. And at every other barrow of more ordinary produce, one of the anonymous artists of the clan is bent over some lesser nurturing.

We pass without buying anything. Yes, Raso needs us. He too is old. "Why did you giggle back there?" Rupert says.

I tell him, doing it again. He joins me.

Can older people giggle like that and not be obscene? To that girl just passing for instance, in a swing of marigold hair blowing straight out behind her. It's not the hair but her jointless ease that I envy.

"See her?" Rupert murmurs. "And the whole windy street? Ah, I love the Village. You can have your twig-and-sand twiddlers. *This*—is environment."

He says Greenwich Village is like parts of Paris, where over and over youth is the crop. But in Europe, much less Paris—I think—is it the only one?

Am I jealous? No—I have been "youth," and could not be so again, certainly not from within. Possibly not even in the joints, now that I am used to their familiar, even sophisticated grumbling. What youth does is to make me uncertain that I am still in the world. This world.

When we stop at the butcher's I choose a brisket, savoring the experienced red of that well-salted meat, and I myself carry it home.

WOMEN GET THEIR PAST earlier than we do. And keep it longer. In spite of which they answer the world more from the flesh than we do. And are always answering themselves there.

I have known this almost forever—or since I began to know them. Yet yesterday was a shock to me.

We were just putting down our bundles from the stores. A sweet fragrance—of purchase and stability—rose from them. And I thought: worldliness is all.

Enough that the meals, spare as ours are, may come on as a clock turns, and rounded with a little sleep—that wakes. To a book lying open, that can expect to be finished. In these rooms where the abiding flame is the apple in the bowl, and the only war is with the ant. While the toilet gurgles toward tomorrow, and nobody in the obits is yours.

Then I see that she is standing with her arms half extended and the butcher's brown bag still in their crook, in a pause out of Dali, or Magritte. They are not our style of picture.

"Gemma!"

I had to call her twice.

Then the arms come down, but inching like a wound-up doll's, and I have to catch the package before it falls. Those merry-Andrew eyes of hers—blank. For a long minute she did not know me. That sharp mind, the other half of my soul's repartee—where is it?

I look to our kitchen for help. A hundred years ago, when tenements could still be respectable, the kitchens were often good-sized like this one, with walls tiled white halfway up, above the deep washtubs and the porcelain-knobbed iron stoves. We came too late for the tubs but not for the stove, on which two generations of a Sicilian clan once cooked. The fire-escape sun, still ours even if barred and gated, is our hearth. The best of our pictures hang above the tile—the Marsh, a Soyer, and the Hopper, whose sad misogynist porch I have marked to sell first, should we fall heir to those death costs, which are now called "terminal expense." All of them, including the not-authenticated Prendergast, are as truly owned pictures should be, a little darkened by the vapors of use. The long white-enamel table, rimmed with a milky blue where the zinc shows through, has two leaves in it, which when pulled out make a sound like a grandmother's cough. I sit Gemma down at it. The sun splashes all with afternoon paint.

In an effort to keep ourselves more forward-looking, we have recently stored away the family photos. That's as near to retiring to Florida as we care to go. I joke that perhaps Christina's baby will want them. The first-born of a forty-year-old mother may well have such tastes. I am relieved that gone too is the snapshot clipped from Francesca's high school yearbook, underneath it the printed comment: *Ambition: "To be a lovely baddie." Jeepers, Frankie, don't we know!* Ambition achieved, I thought as I took it down—the German newspapers take excellent black-and-whites, even of alley manslaughter. Gemma's face was hard as I did it, but not with hate.

And not surprisingly, that moment, as we took our-selves down from that gallery and packed us away too, was when our death dropped into our palms—to be scrutinized.

I think of women as suffering heart-wounds that even men who, unlike me, have had children, would not have. She would deny this, not because she's proud, but be-cause of my lack. She knows I would want everything my span could give, even to the wounds. As it is, I have assumed that our deaths, whatever the body cause, will in the body's core be different. Now, holding her close, warming her eyes back to me, I am not sure. I had never dreamed that either of us would begin dying in the mind.

Then she snapped back. The package of meat is still in my left hand.

"In the fridge, why don't you?" she says, in that voice which will housewife me in eternity, but before I can manage to put the package there with the hand that tremors, she snatches it. "No, why don't I cook it now?" she says. "Hand me down the peppercorns."

I do that, with my right hand. As I do, she clasps both my hands and kisses them, the shaky left one more.

"Since that day in the gallery, eh?" she says, smoothing it. "But maybe it'll pass."

"What day?"

"You don't remember? It was why you had the CAT scan."

"Oh, I remember that all right. Four hundred smackers out the window. What a waste of cash. But I suppose it's routine."

She looks at me so lost.

There was such a day, then. Must have been.

That is the shock.

We watch each other. But unevenly. There are times when one or the other of us is already alone.

WE HAVE BEEN awhirl in the world. I had forgotten—we both had—how absorbing of ills it is to be there—and that the world can be entered by intent.

Rupert bought us tickets to four plays, two off-Broadway and two on—one the kind of musical we are snobs

about, on which we never splurge. How awesome it is
that all over the city these convocations spring up, each
one only for a night—as if the very seats hold spores of
audience.

"No other audience is the same," Rupert said, at the
first theater. "So dearly bought—for some. So much a
birthright—for others. People who *see* language. Who
must have mimicry." And I know he is thinking, as he
arches his white head and the neck tendons tighten: People who may still read me.

Perhaps somebody saw us—that old couple too stiffly
in their Sunday best. For, as if by some sympathetic
twitch in the tough city scheme, our phone began to ring.
I was asked to testify at our community board on the
merits of two projected high-rises in our area, and did
well, the meeting being covered on TV. Within the
month, two articles mentioned Rupert's work.

" 'Seminal,' " I said, "what does that mean?"

" 'Not in the swim,' " he said, before he thought, and
then caught my hands, so that I lost the rhythm of the
herbs I was putting into the potato salad. I always set
them out on either side of the salad bowl, and if I leave
it to habit and to my hands to alternate, I'm okay. I
ruined the brisket. *Don't focus* is now the order of the day.

"It means I still have sperm," he said, jaunty.

"That can ruin salads!"

What has come over me? I have always tended his
physicality, his cockscomb sense of it, with a tact that
came from my own delight in it.

A cowlick on a white-haired man is such a sunny sight.
Now did it droop? Do I want it to?

He took the bowl from me. Actually he is a better

salad-maker than me. "Maybe you don't want a lover anymore, Gemma. It's occurred to me."

I don't know. Maybe I don't?

"Or not in the kitchen." His smile is sad. It's an old joke between us, that kitchens make him randy.

I cling to him, but only in love. "It's rage. Where does it come from?"

His arms tighten. I suspect he knows. But won't say.

What I want us to say to each other, want us never to say to each other, crawls behind my temples like an investigating worm.

You're old.

You're old.

THAT RAGE which wells up in both of us. Why do I feel that if we name it we are done for?

Luckily the phone rang—Gemma's lifeline—and she ran toward it, this time without stumbling. I am thinking of putting an extension in the kitchen, if I can suggest that without fuss. Though when she does fall, she lets go like the college gymnast she once was, so far never breaking a bone. And so vain of her lightness that I cannot bear to point out that she falls rather a lot.

When she comes back she is radiant, as much because the phone rang at all as for the message, though it must be a good one. The phone is your real lover, I used to say—but today, better not.

"Sherm and Kit are in town. They'll stop by."

I refrain from saying how many times over the last few

years our two best friends of early Village days must have
been in town without ever a call. But I can't wholly hold
back. "Well, that's encouraging."

I used to say that I could tell infallibly whether my
stock in the writing game—Sherm's term for it—was up
or down, by whether or not Sherm called me when in
New York.

We grin at each other. How good to feel on even keel
again. Gemma has to have other people for that—for the
even keel. Yet depends on me to provide them. She
won't make a good widow.

It strikes me—why are we really keeping this record?
To find out privately how to survive? Or to make plain
which of us will do it best?

That's a blow. For how will we ever jointly know?

"They want something," Gemma said, after she'd said
who it was. "You can depend upon it."

And upon her. She's the expert there.

I pinch her cheek. "The phone racketeer."

And there they are at the door. They must have
phoned from around the corner.

"Four years!"

Four persons say it.

For the first few minutes, those two look terrible.

HOW I'VE MISSED THEM. Even if I really don't trust
Sherm. And Kit couldn't wait to get me in the bedroom
to rake over Francesca. "We were with you through the

whole case, Gem. Just couldn't lay it on you—to call up and condole."

Not—as I couldn't help thinking—that they hadn't wanted the political association, with the parents of a girl who died that way? Or maybe Sherm didn't.

"Frankie was never political," Kit says. I love her again at once, for saying Frankie.

And for migrating to the kitchen, she and Sherm both—like real friends. And for telling us the worst.

Kit begins at once.

"That picture—" she says. "Those eighteen-ninetyish kids on the beach. In those wide-banded hats, with shovel and pail. Like a border. I always loved it. But Gem, you shouldn't keep it so near the stove. Darkens it."

I know. But these days I want everything in its own place, as first put there. Have to. I never was one to let objects scatter the house—they all hold their places. Now they seem to migrate of themselves—rain boots dropped next to the toilet and left there, cups of old tea on Rupert's bookcase, and once, on a kitchen shelf, an egg, maybe intended for a cake and poised there and left, while I reached for the rice.

"Oh well—" I say. "Probably it isn't a Prendergast. We haven't any provenance for it."

Yet I appreciate she said "border." That's the way it looks to me. She and I have eyes of the same era.

Maybe that's why I'm too upset now to write more.

PROBABLY ONLY Gemma and I, and a remnant few, know how conventional for their time Sherm and Kit actually were—they look so individual a couple now. Survivors of that big decade, they seem now to embody it.

When Sherm and Gertrude and I were young, he used to write about art as if it were politics. Early on, he discovered how much safer it was to write about nature as if it was art. *People* magazine had just called him the grand old countryman of American culture, Kit announced in the bedroom, though we all knew he grew up in a suburb of Chicago. He no longer wears those chestnutty tweeds thick enough for their New Hampshire winter. From which, when in to talk assignments with a magazine, he used to descend on his old New York friends for the night, spreading peaty pipe-smoke over their parties. The pipe went early, once he discovered that the frosted lens that hides an eye damaged in childhood is distinction enough. Newspapers are kind to him because of it; they speak of his "all-seeing" style. Which is true.

In his small field as an intellectual who manages to be popular, I know of nobody who has been cannier on the anthropology of success there. All his dangerous opinions are in the past—but he would never hide having had them. Indeed, his own life is his artifact, and honesty his public profession. He never relaxes that, and is always on call.

Gemma says their house looks like a line drawing to

illustrate the Brahmin life—as practiced in New England. Kit cooks like a dutiful girl who has heard about food somewhere, and Sherm likes his garden and woods almost as much as his image of himself there. Wine is often sent them, by those who like to dine with an arbiter of taste who can't afford to buy. The result is that their raw kernels and thrifty salads have kept them in a fine health that intermittent dinners on the town cannot ruin.

Kit, as a onetime Village beauty and darling of the poets and painters of her period, is as authentic as all the rest. Her sole jewel, the pendant that appears at all functions, was made for her, one notable afternoon, by Picasso, who stuck a bit of metal over a brazier, gave it a twist and presented it—although the story that he offered Sherm two hours of interview instead of one if his wife would pose in a private part of the studio is false. "Who circulated that story anyway?" Gemma asked when she first met those two—and a whole parlor floor of our cocktailing days answered her: "Not Kit."

Although Kit has always been quite matter-of-fact about the pendant's lewd shape.

What pleased her most about the gift, she always said, was that it was brass. "He knew that for us, gold would not be suitable. Ah—he knew."

And Sherm, who at his own hearthside looked like a man who only an hour ago had deserted the desk for the woodman's axe, always smiled back at this wife of his heart. *Did he school her? Or was she always like that?* Gemma whispered to me during our first visit up there, and I answered this wife of my heart with equal pride. *Both.*

I hope this is not envy. It never used to be. Conscientious honesty in public—what a chore. No artist could afford it. One has to take honesty as it comes, in fits and starts—spurted on the canvas, gasped on the page. But in the decline of life, could one yearn for a mite of Sherm's public portion, and of Kit's basking in that as his wife?—though Gemma, proud as she is of me, would never bask. Yet she is the one with the thesis that public approval lengthens one's span. "Those orchestra conductors—" she said once, watching Leopold Stokowski. "They don't only live longer because they wave their arms and sweat. They get clapped."

And the company of those who are accustomed to that can be oddly reassuring. Even if, as with Sherm, the good eye is droopy with pomp. The pomp of modesty, as befits a man who wherever he chances to be looks like one of those old boys who are the native best of some heath historically good. And who in fact has just yesterday been asked what Thoreau would have thought—of something or other. Sherm's answer being: "Even as you and I."

How could I have felt, in that first moment at the door, that they showed the wreckage of the years in a shocking way? Key West, where they used to visit out the winter, hadn't turned them that pumpkin color of other coastal Florida retirees. Nor do they wear those sunbelt clothes that look like food coloring. In the dark of our foyer I couldn't have seen the fish-scale skin and the vein bumps shining through like opals. They are in fact both distinguished-looking persons, still dignified by good hair and carriage for their years, and good woolens. Whenever we were a foursome at a restaurant, the maître d' always led us to the right niche.

It was what they said that told me what the matter was. Or what I at first thought they said. "You two!" they said—and I could see then that they were still those persons. It was dark enough to.

"We too—" Gemma said then. I know her inflections.

So I hear why I was shocked at the sight of them. They have only brought us news of ourselves.

⤬

"NO PROVENANCE, Gemma!" Sherm said, horrified, peering at the Prendergast. Although he and Kit own quite a few works of art, in that Puritan household these look as if they have done so only by intentionally avoiding the ugly baroque, the crowded Renaissance. Opting only, if most chastely, Rupert says, for the hallowed modern. Each piece, like Kit's pendant, has a story, and is so displayed. A one-string Calder mobile, signed "Sandy," with an adjacent photo of the children's party it was made for. The tablecloth on which Barnett Newman one night wrote scurrilously. An early Rothko nude, dating from before the artist went abstract, and this time admittedly of Kit—though quite austerely.

Plus what must be a unique collection of small drawings, plaster casts, pastels, even an oil or two—one of them by Eilshemius, as I recall—and all by well-known but unstable artists whom Sherm had a habit of visiting in their temporary asylums or hospitals. A vocation that came over Sherm, as his books will tell you, when he left off being a Communist.

So all their art has the ultimate provenance: Gift of the Artist. Even if, for more than half of those, the proper qualification would be: While temporarily insane.

"We bought that picture, Sherm," I say. "That's all we know how to do."

Rupert says, "Gemma." But I doubt they noticed. I want them to.

"You don't have to like it, Sherm," I said. "Until you know for sure."

"Same old Gemma," he says. "I only meant—if it's real, you better have it insured." He looks around the kitchen, and at us. "Or better still, sell. You could get a pretty penny."

They think we need money. In the bedroom Kit had obviously thought so, seeing the bed. Years ago they offered to buy it for their spare room, until they found we had lengthened the side rails, making it no longer "mint." "That lovely old tester," she says now. "It ought to have a handmade spread. Like ours, remember?" They have a sleigh bed for themselves, handsome enough but not quite right for a Revolutionary house. "And that mattress. I don't believe it. It isn't the same one?"

Rupert calls it our swan-boat mattress, and indeed it almost is. That deep hollow.

"Those humps are dear to us. I don't expect to change it now. I send it out to be cleaned once in a while." Or did, until the only cleaner who would take it on—a little tailor on Sixth Avenue—died. No department store cover will fit its worn-in curve. But we two still do.

She's squinting at me. "You've kept your neck." She hasn't. She arches one ankle, though. Legs still good. "If there's one thing I promised myself, though—never to let my hose droop. You see them on the street. It's a sure sign."

I've seen them. Old women often otherwise well dressed. But with no one to tell them maybe that the slip is showing too.

"I only do it in the house. These old lisles. I must have had them since the war." Which war? "I like the slidey feel of them." It tells me I'm still in the house—this house.

"We elder women shouldn't keep clothes that long, Gem. It's not good for us. I remember that blouse."

I can shrug that one off. If your shoulders will still take old peasant blouses, why not? "That's a nice suit, Kit," I say. "Custom-made, I'm sure." She would have to, with that belly. Such an odd-shaped little dropsical one. For a minute I mourn for us. What a lovely giraffe she was, once. Where did that neck go? And what an old fool *I* am. Or as she would say—elder fool.

For I know they intend nothing but harm.

"I do have one of those bedspreads," I say. "Dated eighteen forty-six. Somehow we never get to use it."

"Eighteen forty-six, eh?" She looks thoughtful. "Maybe we could swap you. Something you could use."

"I'm saving it for Christina. You know she's pregnant?"

"No! At her age? She must be past forty. And out there?"

"The Saudis have one of the best hospitals in the Near East. And my mother had me at forty-eight." After a string of others, all stillborn, but why say? "Maybe we're late bloomers."

She and Sherm never meant to have kids. If Sherm gives off the feel of a boy born to a large family, not one member had ever appeared East, or in his autobiographies. And in their crowd, in that heyday, having off-spring wasn't the arty thing to do, except by accident—say if the woman in the case died of a bad abortion, leaving some heartbreaking posthumous poems. Other-wise it was culturally tacky to add to the human race. But then they had Daphne—born, as Sherm would jovially tell you, when they were on homemade mead their first year in the New Hampshire house, and "when my good eye was shut."

Daphne took all her father's farm-talk and population disdain seriously, also his freeloading style. As a conse-quence, she now grows Jerusalem artichokes, elephant garlic, and other rare fodder on the California estate of the patroness with whom she has adopted a baby. Of which baby Sherm, in one of those opportunistic flashes that according to Rupert have for fifty years kept him the only conservative to be printed in the liberal journals, and vice versa, immediately wrote: "Our Lesbian grand-child."

Kit's sharp eyes are roving our bedroom. It's an active room, no doubt of it. Twin clumps of books and Kleenex at the bedsides, and a scatter of other intimate objects—nasal inhalator, neck pillow, body lotion—which we use as one. Maybe she can tell that. There's also a jolly patch-ouli smell I want no housekeeper ever to get to the bottom of; it means us. The bed is made up but our nightclothes are tumbled on it. We don't intend to be this graphic but I guess we are.

"You don't mean to say—" Kit says, "Gemma, do you mean to say you and Rupert *still*—?"

I don't mean to say—and she knows it.

We hold it there. Then, just as she and I used to
do when she and Sherm—that rising young columnist,
middle-of-the-road arbiter, and prospective elder states-
man—still dropped in on us whenever Rupert rose a step
or two—we went into the kitchen to join the boys.

GEMMA PUT ON such a spread that I'd have blushed
for our conspicuous consumption if I hadn't already
been red in the face from laughing like the devil inside.
She comes of a tradition that pushes hard on the larder
for its guests.

At first they had graciously said: "Don't bother with
refreshment," then Kit quavered, "perhaps a little white
wine. If you have it." This was before the salmon and
Parma ham and other goods were brought out; plainly
she had thought we might not. Though normally we
drink some mild aperitif, we always keep a bottle of
Quincy or Sancerre on hand for Mr. Quinn, the old pensioner who lives on the ground floor. Although wine is
his delight, he rations his calls on us. I was glad to see
the bottle was full; he's about due. Then I eased out the
Scotch from the store of bottles in the cupboard before
Sherm could mutter, "If you have any—" His mouth
opened when he saw the brand. When Gemma brought
out the cognac for me—brought to us from Paris by
Christina—he would have switched, if I hadn't just then
said, "Oh, by the way, I recall you love *marc.*"

It was the drink of his youth on those Paris barricades

which were to sustain him for years later. When he came back home he brought the barricades with him—or thought he did. To be fair to Sherm, he never thought he would turn so American, and he has taken this with very good grace.

He turns down the *marc,* though: "Good God no, not with my gut!" and opts for the cognac, caressing the label with a leer. "Nothing too good for us ex-Communists."

He means himself, of course, not me. To him my career is sadly uncheckered by the kind of outer history every intellect should have—where some muddle is better than none. He used to joke that I must have heard the quote "To thine own self be true" very early, maybe in the West or even Garden City, had said to myself, "That's for me,"—and was stuck with it.

Doesn't matter. For a long while—my whole life—I have been. And I have said equally sharp things about him. That he too has only the subject on which he has written over and over—the one book. The main thing is that sitting around this table, we remember—all of it.

Alas, including what Gemma does. Who now says: "Is that why when you were invited to the Nixon White House, you went?"

"Were *you* invited?" Kit said.

"Come, come," Sherm said. "Over the dam. Let it be."

I have to laugh. He's a natural pacifier—even when the offense is his own.

"As a matter of fact," Gemma says, "we *were* asked—to this one."

The room grows quiet the way a city room does—just enough to hear the caterwauling outside. Since ours is in a four-story in a cul-de-sac, we may also hear anybody traipsing down the front steps into the areaway to ring Mr. Quinn's bell.

"And you didn't go?" Kit's face is so naively aghast that I like her again. She would go if Judas sat in the Oval Office. And would wear that pendant of hers.

"Gemma had nothing to wear," I say. She does, of course, including some beauties brought by Christina, now all laid by. Only Francesca could persuade Gemma to wear them, taking her mother out to some fancy place to show both of them off.

"Come *on*," Kit said. "I know that fawn Italian suit, for one. And others. You could have asked me to help pick."

"It *was*n't Gemma, *Ki*-it," Sherm says between his teeth, the tone so venomous that I and Gemma have to stare into our laps. It's a revelation, after so long. She's not naive, our scatty Kit. She's a mite stupid—and Sherm hates her for it.

"Your hide's always been too thin," he says to me. "Too thin for your own good."

Too late now, he means.

And it is. For both of us.

I see Gemma's chin jut forward. As her flesh withers, one can see Francesca's bones emerge. "It's not modesty. He *had* one subject. And he stuck to it."

So did Sherm. Back and forth, under and over those barricades. But I won't twit him for it now. For Gemma, using the past tense, as we all can hear, is using it for all of us.

"Maybe we shouldn't of come," Kit says. Maybe she's not that stupid.

"Oh I dunno—" Gemma says, "if one has to hear the worst, nice to be able to depend on one's friends."

She sees my astonishment. She's never been catty.

"Wish to Gaw-ud it could be the best, Rupert." Sherm almost groans it. "But they don't ask me down here much lately."

Then what's he and Kit here for? Spring used to be his season. Any prize committee going, Sherm would be on it, handing out the medals and the money as if these came from him personally, he and Kit meanwhile staying at the Algonquin for free. And arranging for next winter. By which time somebody in the cultural world who has heard that their old bones won't take country Spartan anymore, will have lent them a city flat. Sherm keeps track of those going on sabbatical, and prefers Boston. Kit does well with the millionaires who are going south, or leaving it.

He used to tell me whenever he'd lobbied for a prize for me. But I never did well for him.

"Where *were* you, this winter?" Gemma said.

There was a pause.

"Daphne took us," Kit said.

It wrung me. The way she said that.

Gemma too. "Must have been beautiful out there," she said. "California." But her glance around the room, at the sun now an ember in the west outside our fire-escape terrace, told me she too was numbering our blessings. Including the Prendergast.

"We rescued the child, anyway," Sherm said grimly. "At least—for the time we were there." He shook his head, that oversized benignity which looks so well on rostrums. "At least we did that."

Kit is almost in tears. Adversity never brought us together before. But then—it was never before theirs.

"We did get to London," she said. "Daphne and her
friend Erda gave us that." She bit her thumb. *"Erda* and
Daphne."

We could see that scene—and hear her correction.

Sherm reached for his glass. "Mind if I have another?"

"Serve yourself," I said.

He surveys the bottles. "What an array. And more in
the sideboard, eh?"

I watch him switch to the *marc.* Gemma moves to give
him a fresh glass but he waves her away. "All goes the
same route."

He drinks with the same air of restrained gusto that he
has trained on all the satisfactions of life—and this justly
gives him a kind of rude distinction. His attitude toward
nature supplements that, even if with the engaging pomp
of "Woodman, spare that tree." But smart as he is, one
can't see him in any of the deeper convolutions of
thought. His is a clubman's response to the universe,
socially and physically. Sherm became a link in the old-
boy chain of American letters quite early, and will wear
that old-school tie all the way to Olympus; indeed there
is where he will expect it to count most. Odd, then, that
it's only in words that his shrewdness shows through as
coarse.

As when he screwed his good eye at the bottles, and
then at us. "So you two're well fixed, eh?" His massive
head moves up down, up down in approval, even respect.
"Well fixed."

I hadn't heard that phrase since my mother, the calcu-
lator of the family, had employed it. It was always said of

older people. Those who had money to begin with, or
who had retired well.

It's a shock to hear Gemma and me so described. We
have had two trades, after all, and Gemma is good with
property.

"I suppose we're provided for. Barring the worst."

That word keeps cropping up. I have trouble these
days with finding synonyms, or euphuisms. Only basic
language will do.

Gemma is crouching over the table, in profile too old
for a bacchante, too young for a sphinx. "Where did you
two stay? In London?"

Kit says: "Get me my jacket, Sherm, will you? It's in the
bedroom." She's shivering.

Gemma's arms move slower these days. She thinks I
don't see. But this time she's quick. "Here, take this
shawl." Lately she keeps them handy.

"Thanks, duck." The shawl, a black, white, and orange
wool one given Gemma by Czechoslovakia's greatest
poet when I was there years ago on a State Department
tour, looks garish on Kit's tailor-made.

"You were always full of cures, Gemma," she says.
"Nice Jewish ones, that worked. Remember that mustard
plaster you made for me? That time I caught cold in that
dreadful shack we four rented together in the Poconos?"

I don't remember that—or the Poconos. Were Sherm
and Kit and we ever that close? I am remembering the
poet, his ugly, generous sister, and every detail of that
Prague flat, musty with a brother-sister relationship
meticulously observed. I helped him get to a university
here shortly after. That shawl is over twenty years old,

like our friendship. The poems arrive in the mail, woven
as tight as that wool. I send him mine in exchange. The
world has recently crowned him, but it makes no difference. He and I—and a few others round the world—have
a confraternity the Sherms wouldn't understand. In fact
we cure each other, against the Sherms.

What's Gemma looking so strange for?

I'd lost track.

"We always kept up with her," Kit's saying. "Like we
have with you. Though we never stayed with her. She's
always had some cuckoo arrangement—you know—with
a man. But this time—she wrote to invite us. And it
came—just as we needed it."

One never thinks of those two as needy. Either of
money, or invitations. Certainly the patronage still flows
from somewhere, though perhaps even to the grand old
men not as once.

"Get to the point, Kit," Sherm said. "So we went
there. Down in Wandsworth—not very savory. But on a
good underground line. That's all right; we always travel
light. And when you get there, a very handsome, big
Victorian house. We thought it was a convent at first.
You know, the kind that take in guests. We stayed in
those in France. Plain and clean—and cheap. And this
place was a lot like them. Only British instead of French.
The sisters wearing headdresses but no habits. The
refectory very cheery that first night, but not many at
table. We asked if Kit and I would have to separate for
the night—in France the man of a couple has to go
to a nearby monastery—but the sister who served us
laughed and said no. So we didn't understand until the

next morning. When we saw—more of the residents."

"Understand what?" I said.

"Nurses are called Sister in Britain, Gemma," Kit said. "You'd love them."

"That the place is a hospice," Sherm said. "For the dying."

There was a strange light around Gemma. I hoped to God I wasn't about to see one of those parachutes. Retinal images, I suppose. One of my fritillary umbrellas, as I now think of them. But maybe it was only Gemma's intensity.

"*Is* she dying?" she says. There's a wry smile on her face.

Sherm shrugged. "They let her in."

"Who is this 'she' you're talking about?"

I could hear my own irritation. When I'm fending off one of my episodes I always can. Fear sounds fretful.

One can tell also when people look at one too tenderly. Gemma doesn't. She braces me instead.

"Gertrude—" she says.

"She's here," Sherm says. "She came over partly because she wants to see you. They encourage them to see the family if they can." He coughed. "She seems to regard you two as family now. Her only one."

"*Here?*" Gemma says. "With you?"

"At the Plaza," Sherm says. "Naturally, she needs a—an aegis."

"Aegis?" Gemma says, as if it's some form of medication. Even now I'm often not sure whether or not she knows the meaning of some fancy words.

Kit is biting her thumb and looking at Sherm with

venom. *"We* are staying with *her.* That last man of hers did her rather well. Still does. Though he won't see her."

Then of course I know who they are talking about. There's nothing like old rage to clear the head. I had had to do the same with her as that man. Refuse.

What a gaffe though—the way I said it.

"Oh—Gertrude. My wife."

∽

WHEN OUR downstairs buzzer rang, I had the wild thought that she might be already down there in the hall. She must be ambulatory. Sherm and Kit were not the sort to encumber themselves with a complete invalid, even in order to stay at the Plaza for free. Or she would have a nurse, maybe one of the Sisters from the hospice whom she would have enticed away—perhaps to let them see how we handle death in the States. According to what Rupert told me long ago, Gertrude had always been able to find what Sherm calls an "aegis." Often she ran several at once, all of them vying for her attention. "As if she was saddled with us," Rupert had said, "and she was only seeing how we would do. The candidates will always change. But she will never lack for them. And the attention she gives them is—well—professional. For a long while I didn't see that I was serving Gertrude. I thought I was learning how to live my life."

And in a way, he had. Once, when I referred to her as a femme fatale, he said, no, that soiled old phrase, which reminded one of flashy art-nouveau women in monkey

fur or grand courtesans riding the Bois in Klimt poses,
would not describe what she was or did. "She knew how
to attract men with the fatality already in them. Men
about to brim over with success. Or just losing a religion.
Or just finding one. Like me."

Her pretexts were always reasonable and solidly
grounded. So, any nurse would no doubt learn what
Gertrude had promised she would. Would some one of
Gertrude's many former contacts provide—as payment
for not having to meet again with Gertrude herself?

I of course have never met her. But among Rupert's
friends, the crowd into which I married, Sherm and Kit
among them, she was a constant topic, often at parties to
which she had not been invited, where there was the
fear—or expectation—that she might after all turn up. A
rumor that she might could make certain people—
women too—uneasy enough to want to leave, yet too
fascinated at the prospect of Gertrude to depart. Still,
she must have known where she wasn't wanted, for she
never came. But kept them guessing? "Yes, that was her
quality," Rupert said. "No—I'm being unfair. Or rather,
inaccurate. That was her—nature. You could never put
a finger on her. On what she was or where at the moment
she might be. Meanwhile, over some months—or years
in my case—she might be in your flat, your bed, and of
course your purse, though always openly—and possibly
even at your place of work." Many people found Gertrude jobs, he said—usually interesting ones, always per-
formed faithfully if briefly. "The one place she could not
care to be was in your heart." There had apparently
never been any question of being in hers.

Yet though he lived with her for only a few years, it

took double that number of years of living with me before he left off inadvertently referring to her as his wife.
I understood. I wasn't as wounded by that as he perhaps
thought at the time, or even after so long, in front of Kit
and Sherm. After all, I had had to excise Arturo, the
long, long habit of him, if not the love.

When you marry early, romantically and wrongly, you
may still keep the image of the affair, and of the girl that
was you still centered there, but lose the image of the
man to the life you live with him. I have seen this even
more clearly in the women who stay married to those
men. The old Italian women who were my mother's
friends in Bridgeport, for instance—who could cite every
slightest stage of their one and only affair. *And then, on the
following Sunday, there he was,* they said, their old eyes
alight, and scarcely connecting that *he* with the broken-
toothed husband playing bocce with my father on the
lawn.

I called Rupert by Arturo's name now and then, but as
he became the girls' father, only when it had something
to do with them. And when the girls brought over snap-
shots of themselves with Arturo included I never learned
to see him as that pudgy gentleman in striped trousers,
whose fat, seraph smile was fended off with bank checks.
What I saw, and still see, is the Arturo who the morning
after I lost our baby said to me, aggrieved and balked of
what I owed him: "Couldn't you have held on to our little
commendatore for just a little longer?"

Rupert once rousted out a few pictures of Gertrude.
The earliest showed a girl neither pretty nor plain, even
anonymously median, but confident. Then came a
woman much the same physically, whose sureness has

become meditative, perhaps on what she already had had and could look forward to. She wears her hair pliably enough for any era and looks as if she can pass through any occasion without dressing specially for it. "Gertrude was a type," Rupert said. "Pliable, yes—and unchangeable. But the recognition of that was up to you. And the effect of this could be deep. As if she were telling you, 'I won't last.' Not warning you. Only presenting the fact, silently. But with no sadness one could see."

Her saga taught me something. Perhaps—to live too closely to love, and by it? Just as Arturo's story helped Rupert to be a father, even of the lost son? We were what we were in part because of them. And wanted never to see them again.

So, when that buzzer sounded I said to myself—She means to see *us*. Now. Why?

And Rupert, who had just called her his wife, snapped back to being himself again, looking contrite. He doesn't always know when he opts out like that, but he did this time. So once more she had affected both of us.

"The MacNairs are in California," Rupert says to me, low. He has had my same thought.

The MacNairs have the flat above. And poor Wallace's, below ours, is vacant, waiting for the settling of the estate. The gallery on the first floor is closed for the weekend. That leaves us, who haven't ordered anything, far as I know, nor expect anyone really. Not even Kit and Sherm, who sit there as people do when bells ring in other people's houses—bright-eyed but unconcerned.

"We—are not a hospice," Rupert says. How bright-eyed she has made him, too. A man in command, with not a thread yet lost to him. In front of those two, I'm proud.

"No one *is,* nowadays. Isn't that the trouble?" Sherm grumbles. "For all of us."

This must be how Sherm talks when he gives an award, or gets one. Or at the White House.

"She's doing an extraordinary thing," he says.

She is. Which of our two spare rooms will she expect? By now Mr. Quinn has admitted her and sounded the buzzer. Our small elevator takes long. Perhaps a wheel-chair is being fitted in—or won't fit in. I will not ask those two whether there is a chair.

"I'm not sure I go along with it. For myself, I mean. But Sherm—" Kit is in a state. Pink-lidded, trembling. Maybe she's thinking of their spare room in New Hamp-shire—and summer to come.

How intolerant I am, I thought, about the dying; I should be ashamed. But was not.

"The question is—just what does Gertrude think she's doing? Aside from what she *is* doing," Rupert says, loudly for him. "With her the two were not always the same."

And now I was jealous. That he should speak this intimate knowledge as if it were yesterday's.

"Excuse me—" Kit says. "But are you two, like Sherm, a little hard of hearing? Because I thought I heard a bell."

"You did," Rupert says. "Our downstairs neighbor does it. The one who let you in. But the elevator gets stuck now and then. People sometimes walk up."

"And no," I say, "we aren't deaf. Either of us."

But that must be why Rupert raised his voice—for Sherm. And again I'm proud.

"Though the house is a little moribund," he adds, smiling. And I think: How quick he is, after all.

"Yes—'strordinary," Sherm says, ploughing on.

So this is how he must hide the deafness. By repetition. I always thought it was pomp. And in those days perhaps it was. Poor man, the eyepatch gives him monumentality enough. But now the remoteness is really closing in. On him too.

"What is she doing, Sherm?" I mouth it. "Precisely what?"

"She wants to start a hospice here. And she wants to start—with us."

"With—us?" Rupert says.

"She wants to gather in all the dying—any who are—from our crowd."

In the silence I stand up. I hear somebody walking up the stairs, very slowly.

"Old school tie?" The tip of Rupert's nose has gone white. He too stands up. "I see. I think I see. And you're her ambassador. You've come to nose out whether we are. Dying. I'll save you the trouble, Sherm. You were always a lazy sonovabitch. We're on notice, you might say. Gemma and I. But nothing more."

Kit gives a high tee-hee. "Come along for the ride. Special rates." Then she bursts into tears.

"Kit!"

She gives me a look. Clasping her abdomen. Oh Jesus. So that's what the belly is. She's wearing a bag.

There's a knock at the door. Brushing past Rupert, I

whisper: "It's Kit he's going along with it for." Then I take a deep breath, thirty-five years long, and open the door wide.

Mr. Quinn is standing there. In my relief, I want to go on standing there opposite him, on and on, enumerating Mr. Quinn with neighborly delight.

Even his everyday clothes have an air, the kind the young folks are looking for in the antique clothing shops. A short, faded French-blue overcoat with a pocket beret to match. The mechanic's overalls—from early days as gofer to the racing drivers at Le Mans—in which he takes the garbage out. His little hawk-nosed wife wore a white tennis headband until the day she died. Like Suzanne Lenglen's it was, the day Lenglen won the women's singles. Mr. Quinn played a match or two with Bill Tilden—"before, of course, he turned professional." Rupert says they had the kind of sports-haunted youth on the Riviera that Sherm and the other midwestern literary émigrés never knew, but that both crowds were amateurs to the nth.

Today Mr. Quinn is wearing his Prince of Wales V-neck sweater, into which a canary silk ascot is tucked. If we ask him in, he will be dressed for it. No hard feelings if we do not. But just in case, he will be carrying some bit of our mail that he has spotted as too serious to trust to our mailbox. Today's, a long white envelope, is too big for it, and too square. In order to bring it he has walked up the stairs with his long, elegant stride. Above the ascot his slender cheeks are scarcely pink. I imagine that fed as he is on the well-chosen secondhand morsels I have seen him buying at the vegetable stalls and bread shop, even his breath is sweet. As sweet as the hope shining from his face.

Oh how I envy him, this gofer from the past. He is having an amateur old age.

"Come in, come in—" I cry. "Oh, you must. We are having a drink with friends you must meet. And they you."

He's not a man to make me work at overriding his demurs. And he can depend on me to cut them short.

I introduce him with a flourish. "Our neighbor—who let you in. He is sometimes kind enough to save us steps. And Sherm—Mr. Quinn was your contemporary—in France."

I can see that Sherm expects Mr. Quinn might know his name. Such is not the case. Rupert, seeing this too, is calmed. We exchange what he calls *happital* glances. Happy marital. This little party will do well—at least for us. And will stave off the other one projected on us. Which is what a hospice too interrelated would be, wouldn't it? A death party, with the friends we think we owe it to.

I know who we owe. "We're out of Quincy, Mr. Quinn. You'll have to make do with Sancerre."

After tennis, wine was once his interest. His wife had cousins with a vineyard in Beaune. He likes a thin glass. I bring him a rare one I have bought especially; he has taught me a lot, not all of it about wine. Rupert jokes that the day I buy Mr. Quinn a bottle of Château Yquem he will sue the old boy for alienation of affection. Oh—I answer—to get to that brand will take us years and years, you're safe. I doubt it, he says; I think the old boy is good for it, and we smile at each other, tentatively. Mr. Quinn is ninety-two.

I see that Sherm and Quinn are weighing his position here. Not a super, then? They don't have pensioners.

"Mr. Quinn is our mentor," I say. "On quite a lot of things."

But Sherm is goggling at the white envelope that Rupert has quietly opened, instead of politely putting it aside. I feel his quiet behind me, held on to overlong. No one has to tell us two about body English. If either one of us tried to deceive the other with words, the body would tattle, like a child tugging its parent.

"Is it from the city?" I say. We are our own landlords, under a corporate name that Mr. Quinn, when we acquired the house with him already a long-term tenant, did not discover was us. This allows us to give him certain benefices "by regulation"—a new stove, handgrips over the rebuilt bath—without imposing gratitude.

Rupert only shakes his head mutely, but Sherm, waving his hands wildly, intercepts, crying: "I know that letterhead. I saw the original of the first one given—that who was it got?" He points a finger at Mr. Quinn. "In the Newberry."

Mr. Quinn draws back, blinking, as if he may have brought the wrong mail. "Newberry? A vegetable?"

"—Library," Sherm says in his deepest platform voice, and bends that ruffed white head of his, so ready and right for honors, to read that stiff testimonial.

Then he tries to get down on his knees, or on one of them. I swear it. Oh Rupert, when you come to read this, remember Sherm for me. That gouty knee-joint, which always thought it knew when and where to bend and to whom, got down on the floor to you—or tried. Didn't make it. Not to where you were—and are, dead or alive. Never will.

I still didn't know what was up. But I can savor it now.

How you then are whispering to me, naming one by one your faithful correspondents during the years of your supposed decline, each of whose letterheads I in turn know well enough. That thick paper, smelling of flax, from Italy. The one in crabby French handwriting but postmarked from Maine, a combo that always makes you laugh. The envelope from Paris, always thick with translations, which makes you mutter—They haven't as many words as English, they have to go the long way round—but how he makes it seem short! And from Norway, the most cherished of all—ordinary pad-paper, lined in blue.

"They sought me out—" you're saying, in the weakest voice I have ever heard from you, "they must have testified"—and again: "They sought me out."

Kit is saying to Sherm: "You always know about prizes. How come you didn't know about this?"

"It's not his territory."

I shouldn't have said it. The page you transferred from his fist to mine said it better.

Then Kit says in a stifled voice, "Excuse me," and totters toward the bathroom on her high heels. I follow, to ask if she needs help, though I can't be sure one could, at what she might have to do. She says dully, "No. But I'll use your perfume after, if you don't mind. I forgot mine." Then she turns a terrible face on me. "He wants to put me away early. He thinks he'll outlive me. But he won't." Once inside the bathroom with the door shut, she opens it again. What a crooked smile she had then. "And for God's sake, Gemma, pull your stockings up."

When I get back, Sherm is interviewing himself, going over all the possibles that produced this event, weighing each country, each constituency—as you said later—in a hallowed voice that nobody's listening to, and every now and then touching his eyepatch, as if it has somehow betrayed him.

You are bringing out the Sancerre, and the glasses.

Kit returns, smelling of my Vol de Nuit.

"It's good on you," I whisper, and dare to touch her cheek. "I can never smell it on myself." And show her my ankles, now as trim as hers.

I changed to nylons in the bedroom, Rupert. I'm not at all sure I believe in God. But it was as good a way as any of thanking him.

As for you—you look older. I see that any event, even the best, ages one. Minute by minute the body gives up a portion of its substance, no matter what. Exchanging its energy for time.

We lift our glasses. Sherm is about to offer a toast, to you, no doubt, but you fiercely hush him. The words die in his mouth with a sound of tissue paper, which is probably what they were. "But he doesn't know that," you say later. "Gemma, we're too hard on him." And then you chuckle. "Recognition makes one more benevolent."

But that was all to come.

In silence we sip. Sherm does lean toward the bottle to note the year, but corrects himself in time. He understands ceremony, this he does.

Mr. Quinn is the cupbearer here. As his posture now

makes all aware. He bows to me. Then to Rupert. "Where else can one meet again a heaven once known—except in wine?"

He says this each time, telling us who taught it to him. Each time I forget who. Halfway down the glass he will ask our permission to toast his wife—which we will join. On the second glass, we in turn will propose a toast to the greatest tennis player America has ever had, amateur *or* professional: William T. Tilden, 189– to 19—. He will correct us if we get the dates wrong. We always do. Then he will leave, refusing a third.

But today he is mum. He has his decade's manners. We have visitors.

So it is Rupert who proposes the toasts. "To the champion Roxanne Marie-Celeste Quinn—who once played a match with Suzanne Lenglen herself."

Mr. Quinn, holding his glass a trifle higher than the rest, says: "Not in competition, of course."

"And now—" Rupert says, "to William T. Tilden, the greatest in tennis ever, 189– to 19—."

"Nineteen—" Mr. Quinn says. Then with a shy smile he rises to go.

"Ah—ten-nis-ah—" Sherm says, pointing his good eye at Rupert. "A new poem?"

I stand up again. I don't do much of that, not that I'm such a gentle personality, but because it hurts the shoulders to lift even a thin glass. But I want to make a toast of my own. To all husbands. To all wives. To all of us still extant, harmonious or not, and to all those gone on into the pattern ahead. To the libraries that sustain us, and the vegetables. To this kitchen, a hearth that will vanish.

To the Prendergast, whose darkening cannot be stayed. To death even—that provenance which none will prove false.

And to you who will read.

"To—*this* hospice," I said.

~

"WE SEEM TO BE drowning in sentiment," I told Gemma. "Maybe that's the way to go."

Getting the prize has been like winning the race I've never before admitted I was in. Yet does it come too late for encouragement? For I also hear its verdict: Your work is done.

Still, the announcement won't come out for some months. And Sherm, who had sworn not to tell but couldn't be trusted there, had on the way home from our house suffered a slight—what do they call a stroke nowadays?—"neural accident." "He can speak clearly enough," Kit said on the phone. "But somehow, you don't *believe* what he says."

I saw that happen to my father. Physical loss saps one's authority. Especially with others who are still whole. According to Gemma, Kit is certainly not that. But her loss has been in another direction. That lemony disposition of hers has turned her mind sharp—even improved by the other loss?

"Poor Sherm," I said to Kit. Late in life one begins to love even one's enemies. Though he was never quite that.

Gemma was putting a large yellow tuber into the oven to bake. She's looking sharper but talking less. I think the years make women feel less unique to themselves. She's said as much. Once she was a woman she could recognize in any mirror. "I had a certain flashy reticence. Now I only see my type." And what was that? "A brown-dyed old lady, proud of wearing a blouse too young for her."

What men suffer is a loss of arena. Even if we've never had much of a one. Or even if it's not outwardly true. When the announcement does come I'll have telephone calls, invitations to speak, travel if I want it, and more media exposure than I have ever had in my life—for a short while. But my real arena is my work. And the body crucial to it.

"What's that you're baking?"

"Mr. Quinn put me on to it. Not exactly expressing a desire, but almost. Scrape the center with a fork when it's done, and presto—pasta. Miracle of the loaves and fishes can't compare with a spaghetti squash."

"How is he today?"

"Better. Was nothing but flu, he says."

He had never been sick before, he told us. A next pleurisy could carry him off. But to our relief—for where would this end for us otherwise, there in the same house with him?—a nephew had turned up.

The squash went in. Now she must find another work pretext. Dozens of them in the last few days. Curtains. Duties in the small garden behind the house. My not too dusty books. And oddest of these addenda: plotting our concert and play subscriptions for the coming year. Mr. Quinn's illness, an honest scare, had ended up a godsend. I'd seen it all before. Anxious women pull domesticity over their heads. Or women like Gemma.

"Those big black ants that are coming in from the cellar," I said, "I just now drowned one in the toilet." I always feel guilty—and always tell her. I always wish I were a Hindu who out of religious consideration would not have done such a thing. Yet my hand always flashes out. By what is called instinct.

"Oh, did you." She knows all that. She shut the oven door.

"The ant—reminded me of you. Going down—in such a swirl. And of me. One day the hand above us will flash. Casually."

"You're low, aren't you."

I nod. "And you?"

She nods.

"So it better be sentiment, hmm?" she says. "So let's go *that* way. To the Plaza."

Before we left, she wound her hair up with a big comb. Did it make her older, not to have hair long at the cheek? Or younger—to have dared that high sweep? I couldn't decide.

She said, "It's time. And it should be white."

ALL THIS WEEK we have been immobilized. By a woman Rupert has not seen for over thirty years and I have never met. Gertrude herself never phoned. Apparently that is not her way. If she has a way that she herself is aware of. Rupert says she used not to. We do not speak of her easily now. Who could?

We took the bus. We no longer take the subway because of the stairs, and its general rottenness. I'm stingy on taxis, except in emergencies. The bus is an old favorite. Even at eleven in the morning, the widows' hour, it's not as full of the old as the crosstowns are, and it gets us out, along a route we know so well. Rupert always enumerates as we pass. "The flower market," he says. "Those buildings quiver with humidity. People don't realize. Whole caverns of green storage, in the rear." At Thirty-fourth Street he said: "Macy's is like a large, square fact. Of course it would be. Herald Square."

Then, when we are stuck in traffic for a while: "That British voice that called. I suppose it was the nurse?"

A matter-of-fact woman, the day after the one with Sherm and Kit. Mrs. Acker would be going into hospital for a three-day treatment, then wished to see both of us, the third day after that.

"Please hold on until I get my husband," I said.

When Rupert came on the line the voice repeated its message. I was to be sure to come as well.

When Rupert hung up he said: "Mrs. Acker. That's new. She never took a man's name before, married to him or not. Wonder could that be the theater man? Owned a lot of them. Not in London. Palladiums. Brighton, Blackpool, places like that. Must be. Sounds like her. To have floated along there."

I'd waited a couple of hours. Then I'd said: "You didn't say for sure you would go. Or we would?"

"No."

May one ignore the shrewd narcissism of the dying? Or must one skip to it?

In the bus, when we reached Forty-seventh Street, the jewelers' center, Rupert said: "Whatever she was, she's on Mount Neboh now."

We both know our Bible. That's the one where Moses went up to get the commandments from God. I was glad Rupert hadn't said Gethsemane.

"I'll do whatever you do," I said.

Then we were a block from the Plaza. Then we were there.

On those opulent steps I said: "A peculiar place to choose to die. When you can choose. As apparently she can."

He took my arm. "Always could."

After we got the number of Mrs. Acker's suite from the desk clerk I said: "What disease has she—that she can specify what day she'll see us? After so-and-so many days' treatment."

"Maybe they can't really. But she can. She always specified."

This was more than he had said of her in all the week just past. I know my role. I have to get it out of him, help him to answer her. Help us to.

At the line of phones where you ring up on your own, all are busy. As we wait I say: "That day Sherm told us. And Quinn came knocking. I thought it was her knock. I thought she would be asking for us to take her in."

Just then a phone became free. After Rupert had sent

up our name and hung up he stayed there for a minute gazing at the receiver, then bowed to the next applicant and led me away.

"If that were all she'll ask," he said.

In the elevator we were alone by the time we reached her floor.

"Who the hell does she think she's commanding?" he said.

I know the answer to that one. So does he. If he can ask me that, nothing else much matters. I am his real wife. He wants me to say it for us.

I say—as lightly as I can—"Death."

~

THERE ARE two Sisters in charge. Sister McClellan, the one who called us, speaks in that balanced voice we first heard. The voice of reality, constantly presenting the facts of the case—to the patient above all —and meanwhile making the most tender gestures in her direction, but a laying-on of hands that stop just short of touch. Sister Bond as steadily enunciates their theory and practice in a voice like a dove's—all the while extending the patient the most intimate physical care.

There was no hush-hush anteroom stuff. Gemma and I were led straight in. To the wheelchair. The patient is the thing, at all times. And it is the patient whose task it is to orient us. Our task—the "family's"—is to assist and attend—and learn—in preparation for our turn. Even though the Sisters bloom with a health pink with optimism, there's a distinct sense of "you next, we next" in all they do. The "family" need not be blood-related. Some patients specify not.

"It *boosts* them," Sister McClellan said later, while the patient smiled. Sister Bond: "All available medical treatment is explained to them. They, *they* decree." Often sending away the crew dispatched from Intensive Care.

The woman in the wheelchair might have had a blanket over those wasted legs but must have preferred not. That's the way I see her as we approach. A woman in a wheelchair. The theory is—they told us later—not to conceal.

"Is it you?" she said, and then I knew her. There's not much else left to guide.

Then she got up and walked. She's dying of half a dozen things, we learn, among these too many white cells, a lack of red. This is why they can more or less predict where she will be when. The chair is for her bones, which break. But for the heart she must walk some each day. She has saved that for us.

She told us what she wanted of us over tea, ordered up. "In the hospice there would be other pretties about—like me."

Acker had been willing to sponsor a few other patients over here, but it hadn't worked out, with the immigration authorities for one. And yes, he was the man I'd thought he was. "He's backing a play about our group, in London. In the West End." Though she was no longer married to him. "He was quite willing to send over a few—companions—to see me through." But the management here had also balked.

She's asked me to come "because you were the most honest. And knew me best."

She hasn't yet greeted Gemma, only glancing at her without other acknowledgment, as if the state of dying —or dying in such state as she was doing—was introduction enough.

As often these days when I tense, I feel the wordplay coming over me in adrenaline profusion. What dreadful bit will I emit?

"And I asked Gemma because from what I heard of her she would come."

Gemma ignores her. She's seen my trouble. She puts her hand on my shaky wrist, saying one word to me. "Triolet."

To my surprise, Gertrude laughs. "Never heard that one. But I get what you're saying, sweetie. He's yours."

The Sisters were openmouthed. Their voices blend in a whisper: *She laughed.*

Nudging together, they inch a step nearer Gemma and me. We might be statues being scrutinized.

Just then a waiter brings in the tea.

I feel for the first time that I am in a room with four women. And that Gemma will handle it. The waiter has brought two tables which he sets up at a distance from one another, one in the center of the room, at which Gertrude immediately sits. The Sisters watch her get to it and into her chair, drawn up by the waiter, who clearly knows this routine. I recall that Gertrude could always impose one. The Sisters watch her until she is safe in the chair, their eyes discreetly averted. They are very good at this covert surveillance.

But still I recognize the stance—the way we all look at the sick when we think we are well. I resolve to stare at Gertrude straight on.

Her table has three other chairs. She motions me to sit on her right, Gemma on her left, but I ignore this. I remember that empress motion—and how when Gertrude and I were breaking up I used to wait for that command and then do the opposite. Having learned that Gertrude led you by many insignificant steps to the fait accompli—the path you didn't see until it was behind you.

"What a fine spread," I say. "Though we don't eat many sweets." I reach for a cup, though. I so need that hot liquid repair. The waiter quickly pours me one. He's ruddy-cheeked, observant. I don't wish to clock my bodily processes but these days I can almost identify each—chest, bowel, veins—each an old pensioner holding out its cup. Only the brain will not speak to me direct.

The two Sisters have seated themselves at the second table.

Gemma says, "Why don't they sit with us?" Though she too has not yet sat down.

The two sit silent, like domestic help discussed.

"They like to sit at the window," Gertrude says. "They need to see the world."

"Don't you?"

"I am seeing it, Gemma, aren't I?"

Yes—she has got us to come.

Again Gemma ignores her. "Sister—"

They look up, in tandem.

"You teach—dying as a vocation?"

Sister McClellan says: "Theirs, yes. Not ours. Or not yet."

Sister Bond says more softly: "We sponsor them. Toward it."

Their charge says: "They say dying is a state of being. Just as living is, they say."

I see how they would need to sit to one side, and repair. I want to sit with them. I take an armchair nearby. Gemma takes another, nearest me.

Gertrude says: "Kit and Sherm are late."

Not a quiver from the Sisters, though they may know why.

"I spoke to Kit yesterday morning," Gemma says. "They planned on leaving. For New Hampshire."

I don't like seeing those two faces that near— Gertrude's and Gemma's. One lifting her sharpened chin as if to say, "I'm dying. I can take it," the other rounding her shoulders, "I'm living. So can I."

"The rats—" Gertrude says. "But their ship is sinking too." When I knew her she didn't used to shrug. She didn't have to. "So they've left, have they, those two mercenaries. With not even a good-bye."

The Sisters rise, to sit in her table's two empty chairs.

"No other takers," she says, looking up at them. "So shall we get this show on the road? Go back home, I mean."

"We would have to ask--"

"—Mr. Acker."

In posture too they are in perfect balance, a Yes and a —Perhaps. Gertrude peers at the table in front of her; she must not see too well. "I don't relish sweets anymore

either, even if allowed." She glances up at us. "The stuff
they do allow me—you wouldn't believe. Last night—
caviar. Malossol. Acker can afford it. All right, girls—
cable him."

"To come over?" Gemma says.

"Him? Rupert—you tell her."

"I have." But a woman like my wife doesn't quite hear
that kind of thing. "Gertrude probably hasn't seen Acker
in years."

"Three. The house at Wandsworth's been going for
just over two. . . . Well, Rupert? Go on."

"Gertrude's always lived by projects, for which people
pay."

The father started that, the brothers kept on with it.
Maybe they're dead now but I wouldn't bank on it. More
likely—they've left too. I was only one of her long train
of nonfamily. Acker would be the last.

"Rupert. You're not as honest as you once were. *Men*
paid, Gemma."

To give Gertrude her rightful due, she always thought
up projects that interested them. Often quite charitable
ones, as now. Or, as in my case, the project was the man
himself.

"Generally, they paid to leave," she said. "But Rupert
wouldn't—pay. He tell you that, Gemma?"

No, I never had. How I did what I had to do, on my
own.

I can scarcely see him, that young man whom the animal farm so helped. Wrestling of a night with a calf
getting born, one of my own stock, and with the page I
was trying to make my own too. Which I could do only
if I paid no one for my getaway.

Sister McClellan cleared her throat. Sister Bond coughed.

"Okay, ladies." Gertrude's voice was fainter. I had to admire it for still staying so American. "They want me to remember I'm dying. In the hospice they like us to say that, at least once a day. Even though—they can tell." Her skin did seem grayer than when we entered. Her hair, surely coiffed that morning, hung like rope. Sister Bond leaned forward to wipe her mouth for her.

"I was a baby philanthropist without money," Gertrude said then. "Or just a smart baby—at least in New York. Where they call you 'on the make'—if you make them pay for it. The British welfare state and I took to each other right away. Hobbies can be indulged without guilt. If they're for the common good. And I got quite bright at thinking those up. You only have to look around you." She put out a hand, blindly.

Nurse Bond gave her a kind of inhaler on which she breathed twice.

Nurse McClellan said, "There."

When Gertrude was again able she said to my wife, "How honest are you two? With each other."

"About—living—do you mean?" Gemma said.

"Pretty damn good, I'd say," I said.

"Hush, Rupert," Gertrude said faintly. She used to say "Shut up." Then she reached out again—"Bond"—and Nurse Bond gave her the apparatus again, while Nurse McClellan breathed: "I'm here." In unison they chanted to four, then took the inhaler away.

"Mar-vel-lous—" Gertrude whispered to them. "Marvelous. Stand by." She sat up straighter, taking it slow.

I saw the beat in her breast. To see that in a breast one remembers—is a payment. "No, friends," she said. "Honest about dying."

Gemma waited for me to answer, maybe too long. Was she also—hesitant? "It's not as easy for two—as it is for one."

When she raised her head our eyes met. Gemma, I wanted to whisper, I didn't know it was the same for you.

That we should have had to come here to admit this, I thought. Even if neither of us said it aloud. Turning, I saw that the Sisters were nodding to Gertrude. Who nodded back.

"My first hospice death—" she said. She stopped and took breath. "My friend Ivan. I visited him there. An older man. Quite alone . . . actually. Gay. Kept the ward in a giggle. 'Get drunk on death,' he'd tell them, 'in the company of friends.' I asked what I could bring them all. . . . It was he who advised the caviar."

"Some prefer black pudding," said one of the two at the window.

"Takes all kinds," the other said.

I could no longer distinguish which Sister spoke.

Gertrude's voice was clear. " 'The classless society, old dear . . . quite restful at the end' . . . Ivan said."

"Of course, some are beyond asking—" came from the window.

"—But not you, Mrs. Acker."

Gertrude sat up. Or tried to. The Sisters came to her on the instant, pedaling there softly, in the way good nurses fly. They lifted her up, one on either side.

"I held his hand at the end," Gertrude said. "I was . . . his family."

Both Sisters were now wiping the pink foam from Gertrude's lips. They had an easy-handed system. While McClellan held her, Bond wiped. Then they shifted. One felt how often they must have practiced it.

When her eyes rolled up in her head they held her higher.

"She's fainted," I heard myself breathe.

"Champagne *now,*" one Sister said softly.

The other, reaching to a low shelf on a table behind her, brought out a bottle the waiter must have left with us, drew its cork, poured, and brought the glass to Gertrude's lips.

"Champagne, dear. You asked for it."

"And there's enough, dear, for the family."

Then—with the slightest headshake between them, Gertrude's glass was put down. Then Gertrude herself was lowered flat.

"Why, she's dying—" I must have said aloud.

Beside me, Gemma said: "She's dead."

There was a rattling sound from the wheelchair.

Once more the Sisters lifted Gertrude's body up, this time putting pillows behind it. The mouth was open but no longer producing foam. The chest seemed to be breathing by itself.

". . . Gertrude dear . . ."

". . . We are here, Gertrude. . . ."

The Sisters were speaking in unison now, in the way one enunciates a creed many times said. The words came in such a rush and in so dual a rhythm that I couldn't catch them, and perhaps not even Gertrude was meant to hear anything except that the Sisters were at hand.

Then one said to me, Hold her hand, and the one on Gertrude's other side said the same to Gemma, but even looking at them I could not have said which was which, their service had so exalted them.

Then one bent over the body to say, We made a very good tea, Gertrude; the one on the body's other side said as clearly, Thank you, dear, and both smiled at us, their hands free.

I am left holding Gertrude's right hand, Gemma the left.

Next to me, a soft voice says in my ear: Say something to her now. The other Sister is at Gemma's ear.

Gemma did say something, bless her. I couldn't hear what.

I bend to Gertrude. I see no resemblance, even to the woman who an hour ago had said to me—Is it you? Down at the core of this semblance, though, there must be a consciousness that resembles everything the body was in life. And the hand holds on.

I say what I know she wanted me to. "Yes—it's you."

AFTERWARD, Sisters McClellan and Bond were most sweet to Rupert and me. No, we two must rest a moment before we went; it was always a shock, no matter who. And talking a bit afterward always helped, no matter to whom.

I saw that Rupert really was somewhat in shock; we had better stay on a bit. Besides, I was interested, though fearful of being drawn in—the way one is when one accepts a "free consultation."

"And no matter how the patient dies?" I said.

In the most modest way, they declined to accept my hostility. They had met such before.

"We think we make a difference."

McClellan was not as hard as she looked, I decided.

"There are many like us."

And Sister Bond was not that soft.

In the next room, the morticians were already present. The hotel would have a routine, of course.

"I don't know how it is with your nurses over here." Bond's expression suggested she thought she did know. "I rather suspect they're trained to do a job. A very good job, I'm sure. But with us—nursing is a *vocation.*"

"No matter the specialty," McClellan said.

From the next room, someone knocked.

"They'll be ready with her now—" one said, and the other: "We always see them out. Our people." There was a moment when I thought they might be going to ask Rupert and me to join them. Then they said, in their almost chorus: "Would you care to use the facilities?"

As I said to Rupert later, for a minute I wasn't sure which facility they meant, until they indicated that this second sitting room we were in also had a bathroom.

Rupert used it first, then I. As I was peeing, I heard Gertrude being escorted out. I could think of myself as the surviving wife if I wanted to, and in a way I did, washing my hands carefully at the tap.

"I suppose we must wait for them," Rupert said when I came out. "Only polite."

I wanted to walk to the window to see the view from up here. These days I seldom find myself on such a high floor, and the bird's-eye relationship of buildings is worth study. But it somehow wasn't part of today's deal.

Rupert, too, is immobilized. "Lucky they have a suite."

"Oh, we had to. . . . Oh, we banked on it . . . ," we hear from behind us.

How noiselessly they have come back, how unchanged. How reassuring it must be, to their patients, their "people," that those headdresses never slip. Their uniforms, too, stay so unmussed that day after day, watching from bed or chair, one might be forgiven for hoping that the starch they use is mixed with immortality. Which those soft gestures of theirs will one day confer.

Too sweetly perhaps. Do I find that horrifying?

Then why had I said what I had to Gertrude, at her end?

"You banked on us—didn't you, Sisters?" I say.

They aren't shocked. They must get all sorts of reactions, when they draw outsiders in. As they must do with intent. Have to do, to perform their—job.

"No one else would come. . . ."

". . . would come."

It's only our specialty, their stare, not plaintive, seems to say. As with the hotel and the mortician, they would have certain routines. Deferent enough, say, to address the patient formally almost to the day, then warming in at the death with the Christian name, as a family servant might. Speaking all the while in chorus so as not to infringe personally, yet coping close.

"Well . . . she died as she lived," Rupert said.

The Sisters stand quite still.

I feel their disapproval. So must he.

I want to say to them—Don't you dare impugn those who are not in your sect, not of your persuasion. Those of us who, against all your charitableness know we will die a raging, lonely, irreligious death. A single one, whether or not a boon companion exists. Or existed. You two are nurses, not nuns.

They put out their hands to us in the softest gesture, not touching us quite. As if we need this surely, but they will hold off until we are drawn in—perhaps not by them.

"Dying *is* living," Sister McClellan said.

I wait for Sister Bond to follow with the proper echo— will it be Living is Dying?—but she does not.

Why—they're quite ordinary women, I see, gathering their own strength. Wanting to be drawn in. Having a specialty doesn't mean you don't need to be warmed.

Rupert saw that, as he always does. Did he also intend more? He says: "One day—we may drop in on you at Wandsworth. Never seen a real hospice in operation. I'm sure you do—yeoman work there."

The two of them turn to each other, then to the room, surveying the Plaza's broad chintzes, tireless armchairs, plastic ice-bucket, and the desk's array of cardboard advice.

"This is a hospice," they said.

WHEN WE COME OUT of that hotel, the world that
people call real is quivering all around us. I test it as I
do each day now, to see how much we are still part of it.

"Let's go to the duck pond," Rupert says. He still
misses his farm. He sold it in exchange for family life and
does not regret his bargain, he says, but the farm had
places to accommodate feelings he can put nowhere else.
Sometimes he enumerates them. Ledges the moss has
budged, where other force cannot. Water eternalizing
stone—if you could wait long enough. Manure fruity in
the barn, and encouraging to the rose. Deer pellets on
the garden crop may keep away that dark lout, the wood-
chuck. Birds in the trees chip chip away mind. "I have
a bird goes *psyche, psyche, psyche,*" he told me the first
time we met. "Three hours of that while you feed the
animals and there's nothing in your head but cloud.
Now all I need is a wolf at the door to keep me moving.
Or a wife."

The park pond has been restored since we were last
here. Scrubbed enough to see rainbows in, if the city
stocked them. Across that great frond of trees yellow-
green with sun, I could see another hotel, that thin,
nursery-tale tower from which Christina was married
again. After Francesca went off from the wedding to
sleep with her beau, we came and sat on what looks to
be that same bench. I have no place to accommodate my
feelings about Francesca, so I do without them.

Who could not manage to, with a man like this at one's side?

"She duped those—those nuns," he says. "She never meant to go back."

"They knew they were being duped." They had had that glassy air one has when carrying too full a jug. "They must get it all the time."

"One has to admire them," Rupert said. "But I wanted to be yards away from them. As if they carried a known germ."

"They treated us as if *we* were dying!" The anger that had belabored me at the Plaza now burst on the gentle park wind. A passing young couple, tall, slender, carrying bookbags, turned, then hurried by. How had we two looked to them?

"Would you ever—want to see Wandsworth?" Rupert said low, as if those two might hear, although they were already far, though I could still see how their bookbags swung, like pendulums.

"In my dreams," I said. "My bad dreams. Only in those."

"Even if—we needed it?"

No couple passing could possibly hear him.

"We?" I said—and I didn't care how loud. "We? If we're so sure we'd be seeing it together—then why are we keeping that almanac?"

There were a lot of people passing, just then a buoyant Puerto Rican crowd of all ages, borne along on their balloons and *salsa* chatter. I can ask it quite conversationally. "You are—keeping it?"

He nods. "Though this past week, you know—maybe

since the prize—I've had this terrible urge. To write on my own again."

"Oh?" He wouldn't want me to praise.

"And you know, Gemma—I have."

This is a sacrifice. He would rather not have told any-one.

"One—last try," he says. Then he laughs. Tosses his head. "Maybe not the last."

So—is he in the world again? His world. I recognize a distance in him. Sitting at its edge, I have never had trouble honoring it. At times slipping him the only pencil I had on me, the drawing pencil I used to carry. In the city one never knows when a cornice or an abandoned doorway may cry out to be rescued, described. He's not come far enough for the pencil maybe. Or maybe is already out there, a man on a raft, on a far wave of thought.

Great events stir. Gertrude did that for him. Yes, I can see he hasn't come to the duck pond for nothing.

Rupert had doffed his raincoat and laid it on the bench between us; people our age tend to lag well behind the warm season in our clothes. The morning newspaper, bought on the way here, juts from a pocket, still unread. It holds all the wars we're no longer going to, all the new topics we aren't expected to engage in: feminism, lost or abused children, drugging, outer space. I remember Sundays bannered with marching hope, and our round dinner-table afterward, every cheek in the circle scarlet from hating a president. Rupert laughs when I tell him this; he says all the topical only mutates, as the crowds behind the topics rise and fall. "And have *we* fallen?" I said.

Or he'll tease that women dramatize their lives before they get to them, or in the very act. "A man is more businesslike about his myth." And to him people are never wholly in the world. "We are always one foot out, one foot in."

He never used to lecture. I never used to insist. But today I have to know. Can we go on, in this state of going on?

Parks are dangerous for old people, yes. But not just because we are such easy targets. Twenty policemen could close ranks around this bench, and that other mugger still approach me. I have just enough time to see the time on my hands, heavy or light. To test my position in the world and get my answer. Then it's upon me. A shadowy couple passes us. They snatch my purse, Rupert's wallet, but only to return those to us, with their youth in them. This bench can't hear the carousel. But over there, on the edge of all that green lapping us, we can see that lost Barbizon to which the only ticket of entry is a child. Almost summer now, but my jealous, shriveling body hears the skating rink. Then it is over, that secret assault. And Rupert hasn't heard a thing.

Or had he? He does heave a sigh.

"What did you say to Gertrude, by the way?"

I am ashamed. I should have done better. At a death-bed, after all. "I forget."

"Come on."

"Yes, I have." Haven't I almost, as I say so?

"You never lie, Gemma," he says. "But you sure prevaricate."

I know. That's what I did to myself over Frankie.

"That's because you were a middle child," he says, teasing. He knows how I love that old story, so often told, so pointless to anyone but me. How it feels to be merely the fourth of eight. Even though all the others were only cousins brought over to be adopted.

"Always in the middle of the palaver," I say, joyful to have that child in Bridgeport again recognized. At seventy-eight! And in front of the Plaza Hotel.

"You never forget," he says. "You have your blackouts. But you don't forget. Neither do I."

A child passed, bouncing a ball. I wish it would bounce in my lap. "Do I? Have those?"

He grips my hand. "So do I—you said."

"Did I. I—Rupert, I can't remember. Really. That I told you I did." I can check later, I think. "Maybe I wrote it down."

"Maybe you didn't," he says quick, reassuring. "Maybe I only thought you told me. When I blanked out—on what the CAT scan was for."

We must have been a pretty sight, holding on to each other's hands, dithering.

A young man stopped. A nice one. "Can I—are you all right?"

At every fringe the body is assailed.

I'm out of breath. Never had that before. "Quite all right—" I manage. "Th—thank you. We were just flirting."

When he'd gone on, Rupert has a laughing fit, a little too long a one. We have a pill with us but no water, so he takes it dry.

When I am sure it has taken effect I say: "I wanted to tell her a lot of things."

I wanted to tell Gertrude her whole story—according to *me*. I'm the domestic one, I'd say. I've always known it. I don't mind. He didn't love you any more than he did me—does. Maybe he didn't love you at all. But you made a poet out of him. He left you so that he might forget that. But you didn't, did you. You came to make him pay up. And to find out why he married another woman whose name begins with *G*.

But I didn't say any of it.

Rupert: All I could think of when I saw her was that she was there. Acting like herself, as all of you used to say. I saw that from the minute I walked in. That's why she wouldn't acknowledge me at first. Women understand too well each other's affairs.

She's come to make him pay up. I said that to myself the minute I saw her in the wheelchair. A skeleton in a Paris dress and wearing high heels. People in wheelchairs don't usually cross their ankles that coquettishly.

And I thought: Death is like a man she's living with. Under some cuckoo arrangement. Like: Let me live—until I'm paid.

"So what did you say?" you said, Rupert, your voice dry, maybe from the pill.

You're right, Rupert, I do prevaricate. And I just whispered it. She might not have heard.

"I said: 'He's here.' "

Nobody was passing just then.

"You'll flirt even with death," you said.

I couldn't tell whether or not you approved.

"Oh no," I said. "That was her."

"And you—are you," you said. You tell me that twenty times a day. I never have to wait. Or plot.

Then you say: "I sometimes have a dreadful wish. I want to be there with you. To see."

One can't see any dells from the duck pond. I wanted to see a dell where we might both lie down. And stay to nourish it. "So do I."

Then there were people again and we straightened and smiled too self-consciously and agreed it was time to go home.

"I'll just read the paper a bit," you said. "It's such good air today." You love to read and eat in the open air.

"Wish I'd brought a picnic," I said—and then: "Oh dear." What a thing to say just now. I may even have muttered that at home I had a roast. But you know these mumbles of mine and have already handed me my half of the paper.

The second half. You know I never particularly crave the first. In a minute I'll scan it, to see what lesser topics are for today. Meanwhile the air is good. The sun is slipping through the trees. And we haven't even looked at the ducks.

Mallards, I think. In a sec I'll ask for sure, but just now not interrupt; he gets so deep in.

How they sail, that brown and green pair, so sure of themselves. I sail with them.

Then I hear your silence alongside me. So deep, that before I turn I'm afraid it might be the silence I will not be able to interrupt.

Your profile is rigid—yes. Struck—as is said of medals.
The paper crackles from your hand.

You do move. You do move. You move.

"*What?*" I say.

"Kit and Sherm."

⁓

THAT SMALL double-columned space, bottom center,
front page, which the *Times* keeps for the deaths of those
too well-known for the obits page but not international
enough for the top—there they were. Twice, other
friends of ours have been there, a poet, a novelist. Sherm
would have made it on his own, a benign Grand Old Man
going to his fathers. As it was, the story ran over to page
two and a second headline: "Biographer and Wife
Found."

Gemma and I are to hash it over endlessly.

We have the smug preknowledge of friends.

"They did know the Arthur Koestlers, of course. But
only as acquaintances."

"One wouldn't have to know them well," she says. "To
be influenced."

We have walked from the park along Central Park
South, trying to get a cab. "Gertrude knew them best.
But she would never have considered doing such a
thing."

No, she was queer for crowds, Gemma said. "And had
nobody to double up with." Guilt coarsens the tongue,
and this was still the first shock. Even if our only guilt was
that we hadn't liked them enough.

"Never any cabs in this town in an emergency," she said when we reached Seventh Avenue, running on past me to hail and hail, and fall back.

If there was ever a day in our lives that was not an emergency, it was this one—with Gertrude's opera just behind us and Sherm and Kit gone since yesterday. But I did feel unaccountably frail. As if all my barriers were being put to trial. Gemma has since said that with her, when she feels rickety, it's as if all her boundaries are being nibbled, or sucked toward her core.

But this interchange was when we had finally caught a bus, plumping ourselves down on the seats marked for seniors and the handicapped, although Gemma ordinarily won't sit there. The tears are running down her face.

"Koestler was dying of one of those diseases," I said. "I forget which one." And did not plan to look it up. "Far as I know, Sherm wasn't really that sick."

"No—it was Kit."

"Did she say?"

"Only that Sherm was—hoping to put her away. She meant the hospice."

"And was he—going with her?" Though I don't know that one can.

"Not—just that way. She said she planned to *outlive* him."

"Macy's," the driver said. "Herald Square."

"I can't see Sherm leaving the motor going. He was so careful with everything, outdoors and in." A man with an eyepatch, who could still wield an axe. At times it seemed as if the patch itself corrected him. "Remember what a hard time he gave me once, when I was on the cross-saw with him? 'I have three eyes, Rupert,' he said. 'You have only two.' ''

"Kit always drove the car," Gemma said.

"He built that carport shed himself." With the aid of a local craftsman they called "The Lout"—and paid accordingly. They called the carport "The Ell," as they said the 1790 builder of the house would have, proud they hadn't contaminated its design. Not so, Gemma told me on the train home. Ells were for wintering the livestock, in the larger farmhouses. You can't tamper with a saltbox house; it sits too high.

"All himself," I repeated. How quick are our tones of requiem. And he would have built it tight.

"Plus the storm windows—finally. All over the house." Which Kit, after disdaining them for years, had after all campaigned for. What our austere youth refuses, I thought, our old age achieves.

"But wouldn't they have smelled anything?" No, not that night-blooming plant of our era, carbon monoxide.

"I should have listened to her harder," Gemma says. "I think she had an op. I think she wore a bag." The bus was slow and hot. Her tears had almost dried. Her mouth almost quirked. *"That's* what they went to England for. She must have had the op over there, on the cheap. Didn't they do that once before?"

"Not quite. Not on purpose. But when they were there once, Sherm had a kidney stone." I shut my teeth. The worst of age is its creeping bad manners. That habit of calmly and publicly listing its organs, numbering them. And the bus was listening hard enough.

Yet I can hear Sherm's jovial "I tell you, Rupe, what high-class care. If ever one really needed— And all we paid was two-pound ten for some pills."

"I think the National Health charges now. But of course the pound is down."

Would that be their epitaph? Among friends who knew them well?

"They would have heard," Gemma said suddenly. "The car motor. That old Volvo. In that small a house. Sound rises. Oh, Rupert. How could they?" Her hand searched out mine. "No, it was an accident. How could they have borne to hear it?"

We rode for a while, thinking how they could have, all considered.

Then she said: "No—we forgot. Sherm was going deaf. But Kit—that face she turned on me in the bathroom. Could have borne it." She released my hand as if hers might burn it. "So—it was her."

I watched the people getting out at Fourteenth Street.

I think it could have been otherwise. I think that a double venom kept so long on the simmer might find the joint will to do what love might not. I don't forget Sherm's face when he said that the storm windows had ruined the design of the house. He never cared for the house proper, or the windows, or woman either, except as she served. What he cared about was design—himself in the woods the way people saw him, and on the podium. What's courage, what's compromise, to a man whose life is losing its design? And gradually. Which may be the worst.

Maybe he struggled to get up after all, to recant. Sherm was a struggler. But he was old. Too old to rally enough muscle power to change his mind.

Grand old fakers, the two of them, always getting too much for free. I see them driving doggedly home all that day, in order to welsh on Gertrude, who maybe gave them too much. For last company, they wanted their own. I see them closing the house for good, so restoratively tight. Sherm wanted twin beds years ago but Kit wouldn't give up the antique one. How was he persuaded? A Pennsylvania piece, he said to us. Not New England at all. But I paid for it.

That monoxide turns one a dreadful twentieth-century color. Maybe they forgot that.

I see them lying together as they had placed themselves—their faces tinged with that unearthly blue.

Their bed a sleigh.

WHEN WE finally got home we were both so tired we sat in the front room without speaking. Tired to death with death, from death. Oh Rupert—have I made a triolet? I'm so low. Where's the bright world?

I know it is somewhere. If we can reach. We're still together. And that is the way we should reach.

In the front room I always sit on the sofa that faces the hall. When the cable about Frankie came I went to sit there. When we came in from the bus I flopped down there, Rupert in the old barrel-chair he calls his hutch. From there we can both see the kitchen beyond. Seems to me that if I try I can start up the world again—or stop. The cups out there, hanging so benignly on their hooks, will fly down to help. The oven, when lit, will give out its comfortable first yearn. We all have darkened together with the years, like the Prendergast. I want no other provenance.

And the man sitting opposite me isn't Sherm. He's Rupert—tired as he is, a man who has stuck to his truth all his life. What do such men think when their wives are thinking: What shall we have for supper—one more supper—tonight?

His life has exhausted him, his wives too. One of those tall, spare men, built to bend not to break. Who married all my family concerns along with me, lowering his shoulder to the wheel to take up Arturo's slack—a man he never even met. All those years ignoring the prizes due, while the Sherms strutted the pulpits.

He smiles at me now; is he thinking: That's my Gemma, in a minute she'll bring me a cup of tea.

In Bridgeport the grandmothers of my childhood used to wrap the dying in great poultices of cloth the same dimensions as the body and tinged with some European medicament. It wasn't done for cure but for comfort. I saw one of my uncles done so. The face above the grayish wool had a satisfied mildness, like a baby that has been crying not for milk but attention. I should like to wrap Rupert that way at the end, as warm and tended as I have sometimes done. But with no corner of him and his love ignored—as I have sometimes done. Then, in the moment before—it happens, I should like to creep in there with him. To lie with him, in the box which has no corners. But that's the puzzle, how to put two in that box at the same time.

A woman like me is domestic no matter what else she is—he's right about that. I'm no Kit, but I'll find a way for us. It's the women who wrap.

I know what we must do.

Then you moved, Rupert, not to me, not from me, but

rocking left-right, left-right. Asking yourself: What now, what to do?

And I cry out. Did you twitch to the thought: She's mad now; she's gone the way domestic women go?

I cry: "Oh Rupert, it's all going to be all right. I have a roast."

WE ARE IN the bedroom, this broad end-room stretching across our opposing string of smaller rooms like the top of a letter T. Strait is the gate to our private times, Gemma's and mine—and we've never minded that our nest hangs over the alley between us and the next clutch of people, and has no view. They have less; their building's wall on that side is blank. I have little pity for them. I love that blank wall; all my desk work has focused on it, and the only human noise in this room is ours. While behind me, in a room scattered with our cottony orts and wastes, impregnated with the mucosa of all our cavities, is the view I must have.

No weekly cleaning, on which Gemma guiltily insists, will remove that odor which is not sex, not snot, but the powerful scent of time passing. The years converge and convene here; the air is full of our syllables. My pen breathes them.

Sometimes I write in bed, as now. When the girls were young, each needing a room, I gave up my small study down the hall; it isn't much. Christina, who took it, kept my books as they were and the dictionary on its stand. My desk came in here, but set in a corner as it is, I use it only for letters and bills. The best view of the wall is from here. And from here, as I mused, I could hear even through a closed door the bubbling chorale of the girls with their mother—in those days a convent sound, all seeming well with them.

Meanwhile the bed itself thanked me, growing this hump at the knees, this nurturing rise at the small of my back. Inside the hollow worn in by the two of us. If it grows a lectern I'll move out, I said to Gemma in apology. But though Christina was long gone, I never did. Maybe the bed is protesting, I said to Gemma not long after. Like a foot grows a bunion. But she said— No, it grows with us. Our bed, made with our knees and backs.

Last night we did have a roast. She had put it in the oven as we dressed to go to the Plaza, taking it out just as we were leaving, and before it was done. I don't doubt that some of her myth about Gertrude and me went in and out of the oven with it, and lurked there on the counter in the roasting pan until our return. What did she say to it when she heated it up and brought it out again? —*Finished. And I am still in charge* . . . ? For I could see that she was finished with something.

I find myself staring at that browned meat as if it were the Eucharist. As I get older, the vocabulary of piety takes on a beauty that its possible truth never held for me; I suppose that even for unbelievers this may be the norm. Although the position of the agnostic, bare in the midst of the chaos that tumbles all of us, stripped as the boniest Christ in a pietà but slapping back all sweets or shelter in order to stare at the unknowable, seems to me to earn the most merit of all faiths.

"Center cut," Gemma says, staring too.

I should have thought that the roast would be deadbeat, like us, but apparently one can do what she had even with veal—"If one has the poetic touch," I said, and toasted her in the last of Mr. Quinn's bottle.

She in turn toasted my prize.

"Our prize—" I say.

She smiles like a woman who receives too fulsome a compliment. I can't blame her. Who but the pen and its owner believes that what it writes is made of meat and bed and voices heard through a door—and an accommodating wall. And a kitchen, where gamey shadows merge decently.

Where, as I brew the coffee I make better than she does, she can tell me, instruct me, on what she has in mind.

She's not good at that.

She had put up her hair, to meet Gertrude. I hadn't commented. But now I touch her hair, smooth it, in the grossness of being alive. "Tell me."

"Give it up," she says, tucking in her chin, away from my hand. "I want to give it up. This monster habit of ours. That lives in the house with us. Like a Saint Bernard that has to be fed. When we are only mice."

I laugh, of course. What a way to say it. For her to be the first to say—that hurts, though. For how long has she thought our sexual life ridiculous? "That part of us. That—companionship. You want it to stop?"

"Our *two* lives," she says. "That's not companionship."

A husband asked for a surprise divorce must feel as I did. I say foolishly, "It's not?"

"No. Not at all."

"What then?"

"What do you mean—'then'?"

What did I mean? "I thought that we would fade. One knows that. But never give up." Until the blow falls. On the ant.

"I want to give it up. I've been wanting to. After today—I'm sure. I don't want to go on. I won't. I can't."

What I heard—and in a way am sure I heard rightly—is that she half wants our whole lives to stop. People do half want that at times. And do ask it of circumstance. Even people like us, or rather like us. Friends. Friends of friends.

When I shake her the combs and hairpins fall. She bends to pick them up. "I'd slap you, Gemma. If you weren't too old. And if I weren't." I know whom I'm shaking. Myself.

She's never been sensitive about her age—at any time of it. But for such a peace to steal over her, calming that stretched mouth, spreading the fingers of the clenched hand. "You've said it. Time to say it. That's not giving up."

When I take her in my arms her body feels both light and still, like after sex. Turning in my arms she speaks in the submerged voice we have then. "Yes, let's stay here. Stop here. This is where."

I do understand. Though I can't look at our gas stove quite that tenderly. This kitchen is where we have loved. And can admit we are old. Can say—now let it stop.

How seductive it could be—to decide for oneself. In

the rhythm of that kettle, such a charming advanced one, which not only whistles, proudly clear, but then turns off both its sound and its heat. With someone sure to say, seeing the kettle's cardboard box still on the counter in the brief drama afterward: "This was surely accident. They bought that kettle only the week before."

But that person would most likely be poor old Quinn. And gas seeps. No—a man like me, people like us, would do better than that. Thank God we have no car.

The argument—that ultimate subversion—seeps in slowly. A dallying. Is it more? For a moment I have us rocking in that contrapuntal dream.

"Then—you will?" she says dreamily. "Give up the almanac? It's our lives—but not our life. It never was rightly named."

SO WE'VE QUARRELED. Because I wouldn't say why. Or couldn't.

"Why should we stop?" he says. "Or give up—anything? Why be so doctrinaire?"

That's a word he always uses in argument.

"All that word means is—argument," I say.

"So it does." He smiles, just a bit superior—as he always is with me—on words.

"No. What it means here is—we're arguing."

"A word does change in context," he says, delighted with himself. "As Heidegger would agree. No—excuse me." For a minute he looks lost. "I meant—Wittgenstein."

"I'll excuse you." I haven't used sarcasm on him—since when?

"Both the same period of thought, you see," he says. But his forehead is pink.

"I see—and I don't see," I say. "I merely hang the pictures in this house." It is true that he can't hang one properly. Never could.

"True," he says. "You're the builder. Or used to be."

"True. You always had to encourage me." But ought he to say? "Throw that in my face."

"You never encourage me—" he says.

"To write? No use."

"No," he says. "Throw that in my face. But then—why cut me off—when I do?"

Is that why he was doing the almanac? "But that's not you writing," I say. "That's us."

He is silent for a while. Then he says, in that diagnostic voice of his which always flicks me: "Is it, Gemma? Is it really?"

"True—" I say after a while. "No, I was doing it for me. That—record. And so were you. Doing it for you."

"True—" he almost yells. "And what's wrong with that? Maybe you think I should do the poems in tandem too!"

"No." I can't enter there. He knows I know that. "But maybe poems also bleed away life."

I said this last so low that for a minute I didn't see the slough I'd fallen into.

Slough—that's from my first marriage. The word on

which that marriage fell. Arturo, sent for two years to a British prep school, transacted for by mail, that had turned out to be not Church of England but Wesleyan, had picked up the word there. "I am in the slough of Despond," he would say, when needing to explain his idleness: *"The sla-ow of Despond. Spell-ed 'sloof.' "* Charm, when sifted on one over the years like gold dust, can make one shriek—and I finally did, yelling how it was there he was happiest—bumming off. So I learned what that slough is for me. Or should have learned. It's where you say what you should never think.

A minute before, Rupert and I were only what any infighting couple is. Two angry sofas shouting *True, True* across a square of rug. But he and I have lost the knack of light quarreling. Of casual traitordom.

We had it once. When we were young.

And what does he say in this white-haired quiet?

"No. Poems bleed."

Then I'm down on my knees to him. The knees are no longer that serviceable. How did I make it, to this floor? "I'm sorry. If we weren't in the parlor I would never have said."

He knows what I mean. The parlor is where a middle child, lying under a middle-sized and not too good baby grand piano, can tally the family falsities. And acquire them.

From below he seems like an Eiffel Tower, topped by a face. Slowly nearing me. "Oh be careful!" I cry. Of his neck? His knees? His head? What must he be most careful of?

Then he is on the floor with me, cradling me. As I cradle him.

"We shouted," he says. "Do you remember?"

The girls had been with us six months. We two walked on eggs, cooing like the turtledoves we must always be. We must be ideal, true blue, never blow our cool; we wanted them. Solemn little pie-faces poking from the school bus quick into their bedrooms, we could not get to them. "Manners like contessas," Rupert growled—what had Arturo done to them?

Then one day, a rainy Saturday, the two mousegirls in their hole and we two in the parlor—the sofas blew.

"Can you recall what we fought about?"

"No—except that we both kept bellowing: 'True!'"

And by evening—we were four.

Tea for Two, the girls confessed they had nick-named us. "It's hard when your parents are lovers," Christina said, surprising us at her age. And Frankie said to me, her mother—"It's easier with *nonno*. To be against." Turning my heart black with congested love.

Rupert is watching me. He knows where the thoughts go. "Look at us, on the floor," he says too gaily. "Hope nobody comes in."

Look at him, biting his lip. He knows what he's said. Shall I answer him? Yes, I must.

"Oh Rupert," I say. "Nobody will."

Then it's on us, that fear we never had before. To be in the blind city, under the blank stair—in an empty house.

"Nonsense—" I hear him say, faraway at my ear. "We're on the floor. It must be that we're young."

"Not unless we can get up from it."

Using each other like handgrips, we manage it.

"Shall it be the kitchen, then?" he says. "Or the bedroom?"

"I don't care which. If only this love will stop."

What's got into me? I am saying *everything.*

"It's only—that I'm—too weak for it," I say.

He's pale. "So am I."

But it helps to say. We are no longer shivering.

"Have we had supper?" he says.

I can't recall. The kitchen will tell us, though.

It doesn't. We may have cleaned up.

"Soup on a tray, then," I say. "That can't go wrong. Never has. And the avocado I was saving for Quinn."

"Soup on a tray—" you echo. "Better than laurels. And Quinn can't have everything."

"And a hot bath."

"And a hot bath."

AND HERE WE ARE now, ourselves again, in bed, with all our known humps. Let the kitchen sulk.

"We mustn't ever again, you know," he says. "Neglect the food."

How cozy it is though, in the center of all our medicaments. I have moved my word processor to your desk. You have lent me this pen.

"We must move with the times, they say." You are looking over at your desk.

I am afraid we are.

I hunt the bedside table for some old familiar to hang

on to. The nose spray will do. "Then I can tell you, shall
I? Why that dialogue must stop."

"The what?"

I see that I have named it. After so long.

So does he.

"You don't have to tell me. It's because of the sus-
pense. As to which one of us—will stop first. Or be left."

"That too—" I say. "But we had that before. That's
not all of it." My left hand is empty. What shall it grasp?
Not the Kleenex—too little. Not his book—too much.
The neck pillow, ah there.

"You know, Gemma—" he says.

I know what he's going to say.

"—it's an old story. But I love you. Imagine. A woman
who fends off holy terror with a Nasalcrom—"

Nasalcrom? I thought it was Afrinol.

"—and refuses to learn her Social Security number.
Why is that so endearing?"

"I don't find it so. Does love have to endear?"

"No," he says. "Be ugly, then. It won't help."

"Nor would it you," I say. "Only you can't be. And not
only for me."

He's never liked to be called handsome. When you're
an amateur cowpuncher—he told me early—then they
think you're only a stud. When you're a poet—well, you
had better be Yeats.

I reach for his book. I don't have to open it. *Late
Poems*—that part. I will never be ugly there.

"Collected," he says. "I half wish I hadn't done that
yet." Then he laughs. "What's—*yet.*"

I know what *yet* is. It's like a coda. It contains all the

themes, but is not the end. When the end comes, we will
know that this night back here was *yet*. We will know its
quality.

I knew an old couple in Bridgeport—somebody's
grandparents who were brought over from Italy very late
in their lives. Field work had made them monkey size, or
they were mountain bred that way. Bent double too, and
the necks crooked to one side, the man's from right to
left, the woman's from left to right, maybe from working
parallel rows in the fields. Lucky—we kids whispered—so at least Giuseppe could see Maria, and she
him. We never thought that maybe the looking itself had
done that.

Anyway—one day they dropped—almost together.
Him in the morning, in bed with his nose stiff as a bird's,
her by evening, in the same bed. There's a coda for you.
But they were from the old country. They knew how.

I reach for the Benedrex inhaler. It's for when I choke,
sleeping with my head back—toward the terrors—
instead of tucked toward him. Deviated septum, the doctor said, no sense operating at your age. And only cura-
ble otherwise by some blow to the head? I often fall
asleep with the Benedrex in the hollow of my right hand.
Brand names, little backbones of daily living.

The inhaler is shaped like a phallus; I never noticed
that before. In the hollow of the hand. I laugh then, but
won't tell Rupert why. In the end, of course, I will tell.

"Have to have some secrets," I say. In such open loving as ours has been, yes, one forgets that. But why
should this sensation come upon me now?

He stares at me from his desk. He likes it to be in that
corner. "Is that why—the almanac?"

I hate that word. We must have got it from the Weather Channel, the only television we look at much. "No. Because it was *our* weather!" bursts out of me. "And we were—only collecting it."

"Oh," he says after a minute. "I see." He knows there's more to it. But he won't ask.

I am waiting. I want most for him to see for himself why we must give this up.

Amazing that he doesn't see—one simple fact. Perhaps because he's so much more used to writing things down. And waiting for these to be read. "Posterity," he once said to Sherm, who had just boasted that he himself wrote for that "vast multitude"—"posterity is one pair of eyes, bugged over a page."

Ah, that's lonely, I think. Though buildings can turn lonely too. There's one of mine, almost my first, made for commerce and at best a crowd-pleaser—what they used to call an arcade. But it had a brave roof. We passed it not long ago, in what used to be the outskirts of White Plains, now graphed with mall after mall. It was peeling and beshuttered, chipped like a plate.

"Termites would have been better," Rupert said. "It's only suffering from heartworm." Even the "For Sale" sign had given up. But I remember every storekeeper in it, and the midday sound of its breezeways, that cash-register *ching*. A building is three-dimensional. Whatever becomes of it later, it starts out chock-a-block.

Rupert is staring out the window at our blank wall.

When I first asked him what he saw there he said— "Virgin shadow. And people moving in it." The next time I asked, he said: "Square roots. Of experience. Or of potatoes. Not sure which."

Then it became a game to ask. Then that stopped. It's his wall.

Next to it is the dusty television set. Be careful—we were told when we got it—that thing takes hostages like crazy. But I know how to get any machine down; just don't take too good care of it. Let it know it's in my house. "Poor thing—" Rupert sometimes says, watching it. "It thinks it's history. Like all of us."

This is a night to relish. Both of us recording it, all our favorite thoughts honing in. Then why am I leaving here? Because I am. Or we are. The same as any old couple fleeing to Florida. The appointment in Samara remains the same.

SHE'S CHEWING my pen, I'm sorry to see. It has already spattered on the sheet; of course that bed will absorb anything. I like this word processor of hers and am looking forward to polishing it up, so to speak; there must be some way of smartening up even a computer chip. It was she who suggested we swap. I'd forgotten how machines cheer me. *En avant!*

Last entry, Gemma? As agreed. Or will I lie, and keep up my side of our story secretly, pretending to myself as well as to you—that it is as good to do as new poetry? For the last little lies have indeed surfaced, haven't they? Like the acorns one kept in a pencil case as a boy—and throws out one attic day, as a man.

What Gertrude's lies to herself were I will never know.

But I do not now believe, as I did once, that there were none. Two days after her death, a letter on the Plaza's stationery came to me from Nurses McClellan and Bond. Although Mr. Quinn would certainly have classed it as one for his special attention, he could not do so, having had a relapse.

The nephew, while "a caring person," as he himself told us, proved also to be a hypochondriac of many nervous intentions kept simmering. His mother had been Mr. Quinn's twin—"and also a very declarative person." Reared between those two stalwarts, his own powers of decision have obviously been done in. He runs a small editorial service of some sort and, like his uncle, is on Social Security. "About my uncle—" he said, "anything you two say to do. Doctor recommends a nursing home where he can decline quietly," he said, twitching away from that, and from us.

Gemma has dubbed him Quinling, adding that he clearly prefers to think that all the old couples in the world who live together like us are really brother and sister, possibly twins. "It thins the blood, to be only a nephew, even at seventy," I said. "We'll have to decide about his uncle. He'll sign for whatever, if we can get him to look us in the eyes. The poor man seems to live his whole life in bas-relief." It was he who had slipped the Plaza envelope under our door, Gemma being out at the time.

· For the past two weeks she has been back at the community board. I urged her there, though for a reason of my own I don't want her to get in too deep.

"They love me there," she says. "For being so lively.

At my age. I'm practically a cult. With the young women especially . . . Rupert—how have we been living for so long, without any young people in our life? Worse than fusty. Deformed. You know—I look at them and I could almost cannibalize them. Those cheeks like fondant. Teeth like sharkbone. And the girls—sometimes I almost am the one I'm looking at. I know what she says to her hairbrush at night. Or how she puts on her stockings, musing at all that's coming toward her. I feel that lazy vigor; I am it. Then I see—she's not wearing stockings."

As for me, without sons, I have to think it's still possible to be a man. Because of the infant Gemma lost—even so long ago and not mine—we don't speak of that. Some secrets are mere silences.

Get thee to the letter, Rupert.

In it the Sisters thanked us, reported that they hoped to come back in order to establish a hospice in a building now undergoing purchase "in your town of Yonkers, New York." If they themselves were unable to return, others would be sent in their place, they said, adding: "It does not have to be us personally." Meanwhile we might like to know, before Gertrude's estate lets us know formally, that Mrs. Acker's will was establishing several benefices at the Wandsworth hospice—and that one of these, to the value of total care for one dying person, would in her will be earmarked for our disposal, to be taken up at any time.

I admired the grocery-list calm of that item: *One Dying Person,* underlined. Over the signatures Ada McClellan, Enid Bond.

I neither admired nor condemned Gertrude for trying,

even from the grave, to separate Gemma and me. As always, one accepted her, even at the party to which she could not come.

And when, on the heels of that letter, a notice to me of the bequest came from the executors, as luck would have it, I was not at home.

"Where were you?" Gemma said, not quite idly. Does she suspect what I am up to? I can scarcely think not. "Look what's come." She barely gave me time to look, as if I must already know. Maybe I had left the Sisters' letter lying about? I honestly didn't know. She and I are indeed so inextricable.

"A benefice for one," she said, squinting at me. When she does that, the eyes return to their old Umbrian blue. She is not going to let Gertrude affect her in our own house. "And just in time. We'll use it for dear old Quinn."

And so we shall. When we bring him the news it turns out he's more than willing. "I always meant to go abroad again." He and the nephew will pool funds, so that Quinn can be escorted, which he will need. Nephew, who has never seen Europe, will travel across the Channel afterward, to see Paris.

"As every younger man should," Quinn says, his long bathrobe neatly arranged over the footstool the visiting nurse has set up for him. The bathrobe—a relic of Munich "when one could still go there"—conceals the catheter he has to use, which is why Gemma is not allowed to visit him just now. But he is fondling a bunch of organic carrots she has sent him and is wearing the new ascot she has had me bring. I see that this seventy-two-

year-old nephew of his quite acquiesces to being thought
a youngish man; of course I have never heard Mr. Quinn
say the word "old."

Perhaps he will find the hospice's custom of having the
word "dying" spoken aloud at least once a day a breach
of taste, if not worse, but his manners will carry him—
and them—through their joint ordeal. His world's not
perfect in any case. "I could wish," he says, "that they
had such a hospice at—say—Deauville."

"Don't worry," Gemma says. She has barged in anyway. "We shall see to your wine. And perhaps, when
you're up to it, they'll take you to a match at Wimble-
don." She will see to all this herself, she says. "For of
course I'll visit you. Very soon."

As we leave, she doesn't look at me. Normally we take
that elevator back upstairs, slow as it is, but I suggest we
walk. Slow as we are.

"Gemma?" I find it hard to speak as I climb. "You're
not—ill?"

"Never felt better in my life." She flashes me a sidelong smile. "*This* part of my life."

I see that at the moment she is spryer than me.
We used to be evenly matched. But these days we alternate.

"Then what are you doing—messing with that charnel
house in Wandsworth!"

"I'm not. And it's no charnel. Be fair to them. You only
think so because of Gertrude." She mounts another step
and looks down at me. "No—I'm flying to Saudi." She
laughs with a catch in her throat. "Flying, yes. And to see
Christina." Above me the light from our old hall fix-
ture and the mother light that used to flood her face

seem equally blended. "Have you forgotten Christina?"

You of all people, her tone says. How the small resentments we were never sure of do rise now, in a sudden plague of all the minor boils and warts that middle age kept at bay. So she has harbored what she only once or twice twitted me with—that I was a little in love with my own stepdaughter? *Yes, I'm dotty about her,* I replied at the time. *But only as a father.*

Under the steady glow of the hall light, my hand on the baluster, I believe that to be true. So I can answer lightly. "Do you know—I had. Forgotten. For the moment. But only as fathers do."

And she believes me. But on the landing she stops. "Now you tell me. What you've been up to. *I've* told you. What I."

So I tell her—if only part of it. "I've bought some land. Not far from where the farm used to be. Of course that's all built over now, that near to town. But there was a patch—not too many miles north of it."

She smiles—and says softly: "Ducks?" And when I answer: "River. Not lake," she nods. That is all, positively all. She is wonderful. I have the sense that at times like these, moving back and forth between innuendo commanded from a lifetime of dual experience, we are each other's bootstraps. By which we shall lift and lift one another. And fall. But not do worse than—fall.

HOW FAR one can see across a room—and when one is not in bed with the person opposite! Almost as far as one will see on the new farm, looking back on the old?

I am getting dangerously fond of this processor, which can transcribe my thoughts faster than I can feel them. And digest them, to conclusions still ahead? I have an idea—or maybe it does—that give it a hint and it could absolve me of my secrets altogether.

While Gemma over there holds my old Parker pen loose and absently in her hand. I used to have trouble finding the rubber tubes for it, the last of them discovered in a slice of a store way west on Fourteenth Street, whose owner sells parts for all superannuated desk material with as confidential an air as if he is a "fence" for thieves. But not long ago I read that savvy Harvard Business School graduates are affecting pens like mine. It runs on ink.

Gemma, I fancy, is afraid of it—and maybe rightly. If ever I'm unable to wield a pen except through her, would that old gutta-percha case let loose all the leftover in both of us, all the unsaid? Or celebrate that—and why not? But women, who initiate so many of the formalities, are as superstitious of them.

Meanwhile, how busy she has been. Mr. Quinn and his Quinling are gone. His apartment will be kept for him, for as long as he signifies, but to his delight, Gemma, who helped them pack, encouraged him to take his entire wardrobe, admiring the elegantly patterned jackets or yellowed white linens as they emerged. "You'll need all those changes," she assured him. "I understand that the establishment is run as much as possible like a hotel. Actually they have a wine list. But you might be of some help to them there."

He gave her one of his wife's headbands, lavender-spotted, which she wore to the airport. She is so thin now that any gewgaw becomes her. Loitering behind the wheelchair, as Nephew pushed and she trotted brightly alongside, I felt quite *de trop,* Gemma's coy glance over her shoulder telling me that this was intended. Just before they embarked she handed the nephew a carefully wrapped sack from our good liquor store, saying, "Once he's installed, open this."

In the cab going home she rested her head on my shoulder. "Want to know what the bottle was?"

I remembered my crack about suing the old boy for alienation of affection. "No need. Château Yquem."

Her chuckle will never tell me. I hoped it was that, for the sake of both Quinn and us. At our age it's good to see sentiments come full circle, even repartee. And coyness is the parsley on the plate.

When we came home we broke out a more ordinary bottle for ourselves, and ate well, but no coziness could hide a new quality in the silence of the house. There's an intercom on which we can respond to the downstairs buzzer; there always was. But no one will now intercede for it or overrule it. The door down there will flap outward only for ourselves and unlock only to our key. Our tenant made no more noise than a mouse, but a home that knows it has a pet mouse is marked by a quiet that is different. Again it is the weekend, with all our tenants absent. Outside, the city cries and calls in a rhythm woven into the silence like in a tapestry. Inside, this floor-through that once rang with schoolgirls is like a fortress from which the sentries have departed. For the first time in all the years of our tenure here we are totally alone.

Gemma too appears to be listening, staring at me as if it's my turn to speak. I do.

"Is it me you're leaving? Or the house? Or us as we are?" I know the answer perfectly well: All three of us. With the possible addition of herself alone, as well. As what people do flee—geographically?

It seems she has already bought her plane ticket to Saudi.

"I took the money I saved up for Francesca's emergencies."

She always saved for those, pinching it from the few architectural assignments she still gets—as only fair to me, she would say, although all our other accounts are joint.

Her left hand flumps open—in memoriam? The inhalator rolls away—no more need for it now? She's scarcely mentioned the baby to come, or even Christina—are they merely a direction to go?

"And do I follow you?" I said.

Her look is sidelong, then a full-throated stare, the breasts raised, shoulders contracted backward in an agony of acceptance, the same stance she gave me the night we met, from her bed. I know every cell of this woman, her indecisions and her certainties, yet I do not dare touch her. Age makes another person out of the dearest bride.

But if this is coquetry, it's the deepest flirtation of our lives.

Why won't she tell me why she really wants to give up this record of us? Which she had at first entered as engrossedly as I.

Why doesn't she ask me why I bought that land?

Just so she dragged her right hand farther behind her in the bedclothes, all those years ago, and the flung hairbrush rolled from the bed and fell. Now the pen drops from that same hand into the bedclothes. Both hands are now empty, as back then. And now my arms should grip her waist, my head should be on her breasts.

Instead, I am at her desk. She won't have to tell me again, to stop the lovemaking. Across the length of a room come the changes, the deepest ones. I could feel this one in my own cells. No bones creaking, no blood ebbing. Just that slow jolt, repeated in the brain, when the carriage stops, has stopped.

But she can never be a stranger to me. I'll follow that.

"I'll use the rest of the money *I* was saving for Christina." She would know that's how I bought the land. But not what I'd been saving the balance for.

She doesn't even nod. "What I wrote. I never printed it up."

I exchange stares with the word processor. One couldn't call it a glare, on either side. In my boyhood I was fond of a drawing I had of Aladdin's lamp. The genie had risen from the spout, long and elastic, but only half formed.

A sharp twiddle on those fully formed keys there, and we're free of it. Her record.

Is she suggesting that I—? She's capable of anything.

On the bedside table, next to my book, is my own sheaf in its thick envelope, right under the fresh page she'd been scratching on. The envelope is one of those heavy-grade mud-colored packets carried by lower-class European diplomats perhaps, or maybe their spies; I get them from the last of the corner drugstores down here. Inside it, the sheets I write on are a thin tan, as tough and resistant as the town that makes them.

"Tearing paper is harder. That paper. I used the Italian. Are you sure you're up to it?"

She stretches out a defiant hand. It touches my book instead. She draws the hand back.

"And why can't we each destroy our own?" I shouted it.

"Because—we wouldn't," she whispered. "Or you— wouldn't. And maybe not I."

A sheaf, a whole sheaf. It's like that litany the Jews say—at Passover is it?—A loaf, a loaf, something like that. Meaning, it's what you have on hand, to offer?

Plus all I meant still to say. Of how age isn't at all as I thought it; a menopause of the life principle, a general decline. Or a birthing—by the bodily pain Gemma and I haven't had much of yet—back into the general delivery.

It's like life. A total disease. Or parade. I think the Sisters, those nuns, would understand what I mean.

Whatever it is, it's worthy of being spoken of every day. But it's also a nitpicker's paradise.

For Gemma grabs up my sheaf, tumbles out of bed, and brandishes it with that triumphant air women have when they're forcing themselves to do what they'll regret. "Here. Do it, then. And I'll do mine."

As she advances I see how the pretty feet have grown greenish with veins, and the toenails have yellowed to horn. Guilt says I should be ashamed to observe this; age says I have that right. They are like my own. These days I see everything of the flesh so near. And all of it as my own flesh—even children. What is happening to us—is it as great as anything in literature—and what any child can see?

Close she comes, closer—will she touch me first, or this machine? A misnomer, as I know. What's sitting on the desk here is a progression almost without matter, of replicas without devotion to any original. A succession of tumbrils, of many little tipcarts, ready to thrill once and deliver their load—to the abyss.

"What's that blot on the back of your gown?"

She turns slowly, sneaking up on it the way women do when they fear that menstrual blood has seeped through. "There's no blot on my dress, Rupert . . . *Rupert!*"

I have to brush away auras to see it, but it's there.

"Yes there is. And on the bed, too. That great inky blot."

Fritillary shapes fly there to mask that great spreading, big as a third body on the bed that is empty of us.

"My pen, my pen bleeds for us," I hear myself cry. Then I fall.

As one does knowingly, lightly through cloud.

HOW MUCH LATER did I wake to find the two of us on the floor, her arms nursing both of us, below her tranced stare?

I saw again with full clarity now. But she was dead away, blank among her nimbuses.

"What was I going to do just now, Gemma? A minute ago?"

She is facing our wall, blued now with dusk. Or was it now early morning?

Did she get to the desk before I blanked out? I thought not. My papers are where she must have dropped them. In exchange for me.

I am weak, but nothing I now confront is speckled or shaded beyond the ordinary. Her arms are rigid, thralled, but strong. And when addressed during these lapses, she will often answer to the point, as a person in full command might do, though absently. When I tell her doctors this, they shrug—and don't credit my clarity.

We are one person now, made up of two. Advantage must be taken of it.

"Gemma. You were going to tell me. Why must we destroy it."

"Destroy what?"

"What we wrote."

She is silent, struggling. "Oh that." She shrugs—but not with the minimal tic of her doctors. A long-hoarded, slow rise of the shoulders, arms crossed, hands nursing her elbows. "Because—" She gets it out quite tonelessly. "Only one of us will be—read." She arches toward that wall as if to a person, her hands slipping to the floor. "No! That's not what I mean." Her palms realize what they are pressing. She turns them up, spreading her fingers. "I mean—one of us will be left unread, that's all. . . . What am I doing on the floor? . . . Rupert—what are you?"

I could lie, pretend. I could say that we fell out of bed—wrapped in a mutual dream. Once in the early years we did do that. After sex and sleep it was, and we awoke laughing. On this same floor. I see the two of us, ruddy and moist.

But with what is creeping toward us, better to be as honest as we can. There'll be enough clouding up. "I fell—in one of my attacks. You came after me. We must have both conked out."

"Get back in bed!" she says—from the floor. That's my Gemma.

I would prefer to stay at the desk. But she's herself again. So am I. These are the moments that must be saved. The ones when we are both ourselves.

"Bed welcome," I say, once we are in it. "Hand me my pen."

She sighs luxuriously, handing it to me. "And there is no—blot—now?"

"None." But for a while, I don't write.

One half of our joint record will be read, by the survivor. The survivor's half will not be read, by the dead.

How simple. The builder saw, three-dimensionally, what this apostle of print did not.

One of us will be read. The other never will be. My heart is wrung for both of them.

But isn't that what always happens? One half a couple has to go on, unread from then on. And is that why some people—Gemma—raging against that impasse, want willfully to destroy? Before destiny can get to them?

"I can afford to be—lost," I say. "I already have a record—of sorts. But yours must not be." It might never have anyone else, except me.

"I don't mind. I won't have said that much you haven't. Above *our* lives. We talk so alike now." She flashed me a humble glance. "And print—it's not my medium." Her voice wavered on that, her hand hovering over the night table, seeking some medicament. Was she thinking of that White Plains relic of her medium? "Let's have breakfast!" she said, and sprang out of bed.

"But—" I point to that wall, on which long shadows are converging. It's not morning after all. That blue was dusk.

"I know. But we can choose now, you know. We can do anything."

"How right you are."

When she comes back with her laden tray the room is in half-dark. I switch on the bed lamps, then turn them off again. Aided by the reflected streetlamps, this seductive semidark will last for some time. Half the poems in that book were written in it. The bedlights are on a stat that at a flick will light both, or one and one, and grade each down as wanted. This house is old but has its modernities—quite a few—that I have never thought of as crude. They are hers—her words.

Still, we must get out of this house. So much of the world only now and then laps at its edges. Black water, when it does come, seeped from other people's basements—why do I think that? When our own basement is as dry as a bone.

Above the bed tray, that old side-pocketed one whose wicker she scrupulously repaints, telling me meanwhile how much the catalogues now charge for them, her face is serious. "Look what I found when I moved the tray." We haven't used it recently. Except after sex, I don't relish meals in bed.

I turn over the packet of cigarettes, Benson & Hedges, in their smart, uncrumpled pack, only one gone. Kit's, her trademark, for all the years we knew her. Plus those butane lighters, scattered over her friends' houses like seed.

"No lighter?"

"No. I looked."

The omelet is as plump as on our first morning together, the espresso as strong. Our digestions have lasted. Kit's cigarettes have been dropped in the melee of provender on the night table. I pick them up. "She didn't smoke while she was here."

"She knows we don't now. Knew."

Haven't for twenty years. I quit first, then Gemma. I take out two cigarettes. I recall this brand as ovals; these are not. A pity. "Let's."

In memoriam? She doesn't have to say.

Our smoke goes straight up. And still makes us cough. Carefully we grind out the stubs.

"Gertrude's gathered in the crowd," Gemma says. "In her own way."

I sit up hard. "Never. Not us. It's on me—whatever we do now. And on you. And Gemma—listen." Now is the time. "You remember that water system I had at the farm—the old ram?" I lean back on the pillow, dreaming it. "What a sound it made."

She nods that rhythm, and herself, into the crook of my arm. " 'Like circumstance,' you said, 'nudging destiny.' I was never sure what you meant."

Nor was I. But in those words I could hear the ram. "The new land has water for such a system. And a ravine just right for it. No pond yet—but easy. Will you build me a house on it?"

How quiet she is. Then she reached up to stroke the cords of my neck, all too prominent these days. "You're my building," she whispered. Then she rolled over on her face. Against my breastbone, the dry sobs came, deep and regular, a sound like quicksand sucking in. That I had pulled her from?

I can't sob. But I had to get up and pee or else wet the bed. The body calls the tune these days. And who says a man don't pee sitting down?

When I return she's flung back against the headboard like a Nike, eyes closed. "I'm seeing it. Drawing it." The tears seep down. *"Psyche, psyche, psyche,"* she says, eyes fast shut. "That's a bird."

At her side of the bed the fancy Roman-numbered clock the girls brought us one year from Italy ticks on.

It came with its own gift card, on which the Latin text, *Ars longa et vita brevis est*—in my youth usually translated as "Art is long and time is fleeting"—was inscribed in both the Latin and the Italian. Under which someone, I suspect Arturo, had painstakingly lettered: "Art is long going, time fleets." At the first sight of which, I am not ashamed to say, I added: "On little cats' feets." But the clock, still baring its gaunt numerals like a patrician with black teeth, ticks on. Perhaps we should sell it with the house.

Can she build the new one? Her blueprints were always as beautiful as lace. No contractor ever had trouble with them. But there's more to it than drawing. We shall have to act together—as one. As the single, slightly damaged persona we now are. Taking care as we can that the Rupert half and the Gemma half are not *non compos mentis* at the same time. Plato would be interested.

Funny—how the schoolboy Latin filters back, tasting of penny candy and smelling of Father Schlegel as he whiffed past the one little Protestant. I shall be bobbing for apples next, with childhood's long scoop. But the meditation that comes with these penny memories is plenty adult, staring as it must into death's eyeless eye.

Gemma's eyes are open now.

"We must use the whole house of ourselves," I said. "Not close up room after room in us, and live in one. As old people do. And we must let history in. We tend to stop it at the door."

"I shall miss this kitchen," Gemma says. Had she misunderstood my meaning? No, she had not. For then she giggled. "But maybe the Prendergast will turn real."

Lazily now, she watches as I write, each of us feeling her mind stream into mine. "What's that you're writing?" she says. Is she teasing?

"An—archive." The end of one.

"Ah—yes that's it," she says. "Not an almanac. Archives are not so—relentless, day after day. They—accumulate."

"And can be printed up."

When I scold I can see in her face that waif under a piano, her mouth an overturned U. "I did print up a copy of my half, just in case. And put it in the bank, for Christina."

"Just in case?" I had to smile. Just in case she was the one to survive? No smiling matter. But I have to. "Well."

"I knew you wouldn't mind."

"No." Scarcely.

"I mean—if you could have known."

"No." It strikes me that the boundaries between what one will or will not know—and when—are gently blurring. "No—I wouldn't have minded Christina."

She has to smile too, but there's no malice in it. Acceptance, rather. "Well."

And then, right here on the page, this new cheaper lined paper so simple to destroy or keep, a true solution comes to me. As it must have come to Sherm and Kit, in their way. As to all death's apprentices. How to end. How to go on.

"We'll read them both, tomorrow. Side by side, here. I—yours. You—mine."

Her hand steals into mine. "Or—on the plane. Rupert—I bought you a ticket too."

After a minute she says: "Are you surprised?"

Not really. Not if I look at our lives straight. Or at our generation.

"Secrets—" she says, "have you minded them much? As—breaches of promise?"

Absolutist that I have been, I have minded—some. Even though I too have them. I read a page or two of her record before it left the house. "I try not to. After all, what did we promise? Faith—without works."

I see her nod through the shadow. At this hour our only light is as we like it best—the tenacious rose-prickling of the city, from outside. On a nest.

"And do you mind?" I said. "My secrets?"

"No." She said it faintly, sleepily. "They sparkle—in the dark."

That will be the last thing she says, I thought—the last I will have to record. Then her voice came strong—"And in the new house I'll say *Living*—at least once a day"— and faded.

We are all apprentices. When looking into the eyeless eye. I reach across her body for the inhalator, holding it like a weapon.

I see the pond, jeweled with duck. The ram rides in, and retracts. *Whoom,* a-duh. A-duh—*whoom.* I hear the moss budge. Our nest here still smells of the sexual. I touch her there.

So the blank wall darkens. As we ride toward it.

Our bed a skiff.

As any child can see.

ABOUT THE AUTHOR

HORTENSE CALISHER *is currently at work on her twelfth novel and a collection of essays. Formerly the president of P.E.N., she is now president of the American Academy and Institute of Arts and Letters.*

Born in New York City, Hortense Calisher lives there and in upstate New York with her husband, the writer Curtis Harnack.